Eternity

Also by Heather Terrell

Fallen Angel

HEATHER TERRELL

Eternity

A Fallen Angel Novel

An Imprint of HarperCollinsPublishers

HarperTeen is an imprint of HarperCollins Publishers.

Eternity

Copyright © 2011 by Heather Terrell
www.epicreads.com

Library of Congress Cataloging-in-Publication Data
Terrell, Heather.
 Eternity : a Fallen angel novel / Heather Terrell. — 1st ed.
   p. cm.
 Summary: Ellie and Michael's love is tested as they enter a battle
between fallen angels that could destroy the world.
 ISBN 978-0-06-196571-5 (trade bdg.)
 [1. Supernatural—Fiction. 2. Angels—Fiction. 3. Good and evil—Fiction.
4. Love—Fiction. 5. High schools—Fiction. 6. Schools—Fiction.] I. Title.
PZ7.G7487Et 2011   2011001883
[Fic]—dc22   CIP
                                                            AC

Typography by Tom Forget
11 12 13 14 15   LP/BV   10 9 8 7 6 5 4 3 2 1

First Edition

For Jim, Jack, and Ben, who make everything possible

"The Elect One shall arise. . . ."

The Book of Enoch 51:1

PROLOGUE

Michael and I stood hand in hand, the world around us nearly dark. No moon, no stars, no man-made light illuminated the night sky. It was me and Michael, alone in the blackness.

I knew we stood on the beach, even though I could see only the barest outline of the shore. I heard the crash of the waves before us, and I felt the rough, rocky sand under my bare feet.

I sensed that we were waiting. The air was heavy with our anticipation, and I felt the tension of Michael's grip. What we were waiting for, I wasn't sure.

A hint of light appeared on the horizon. The tiniest sliver of gold, yet it was enough to brighten the terrain. White-capped waves appeared before us, and steep cliffs took shape behind us. I could discern Michael's pale blond hair, green eyes, and beautiful face. I saw now that we stood in a familiar cove. Ransom Beach.

Soon, the sun began its ascent in earnest. As if a lens had been focused, we saw fine details of the landscape, even the heather growing in the tiny niches of the cliffs. The world looked brighter, clearer. More perfect.

I knew then that we had been waiting for this precise moment. I turned to Michael, and we beamed at each other in joy and understanding.

Then somewhere, in the far, far distance, I heard the faint ringing of a bell. I tried to ignore it, but it grew louder and more persistent. Somehow, I knew that it was calling me back. Calling *us* back.

From his expression, I knew that Michael had heard the bell toll and comprehended its meaning as well. The smiles disappeared from both our faces. Neither of us wanted to go. Yet we knew we must. We were being summoned.

We tightened our grip on each other and closed our eyes.

And we ascended.

ONE

The end of time does not start off as, well, as apocalypti-
cally as you might think.

The alarm went off at 6:45 like it did every school morning. As usual, I hit the snooze button once, then twice. I
needed a little more sleep to banish that haunting dream of
me and Michael standing on Ransom Beach. Finally, on the
third irritating ring, I switched off the alarm.

I opened my eyes a crack.

Instead of facing Armageddon, I woke up in my bed
at home as if it was a normal day. How had I gotten to
Tillinghast, Maine, from Boston? My last memories were
of Quincy Market and Michael, and, oh God, Ezekiel.

I pushed aside my heavy quilt and sheets, and lowered
my feet to the cold wood floor. Shivering in the crisp fall
morning, I walked over to my desk to grab my black bag,
the one I took with me everywhere. Surely it contained
some evidence of my trip to Boston, some explanation of

how I got back from there.

I rifled through it but couldn't locate a single thing proving I'd been to Boston or showing how I got from there to here. Not a train ticket stub, not a random coffee shop receipt, nothing with a Boston address on it. My bag contained only the usual assortment: books, scraps of notes, cell phone, and wallet.

Was the trip to Boston a dream? And if that was a dream, was all the stuff about the Nephilim and the Elect One a dream? Had I only imagined the flying and the blood? Was my relationship with Michael a fantasy too?

Still, I couldn't shake the unsettling feeling that the Boston trip was *not* a dream. Part of me longed to call Michael and ask him. But how could I do that? Would he think that his girlfriend had gone absolutely crazy? And that was assuming I actually *was* his girlfriend and I hadn't dreamed that part up too. I couldn't take the chance.

I decided to head downstairs to grab breakfast and talk with my mom. If I'd been in Boston with Michael yesterday, she would *definitely* bring it up. I would use her as my litmus test for what was real and what was not.

As I left the relative safety of my bedroom and stepped out into the hallway, I spotted a photo stuck in the corner of my mirror. I drew closer and realized that it was a picture of me and Michael from the fall dance. I sighed in relief. At least I hadn't imagined my entire relationship with him.

But still, there was this whole Nephilim and Elect One business to sort out. Yes, I told myself, a brief chat with my mom was just the thing to sift through my confusion. Yet, as I placed my hand on the banister leading downstairs, I was suddenly certain that this wasn't an ordinary day, that there would be no more ordinary days.

Two

My mom was acting perfectly normal. Almost too normal. Or maybe I was seeing her through the lens of my own uncertainty.

From across the kitchen counter, she asked in surprise, "Ellie, why are you still in your pajamas? You have to leave for school in five minutes."

I glanced around the kitchen, which appeared exactly the same as always. My mom looked like she usually did too. There she stood, unflappably cheerful and unnaturally gorgeous. Dark, lustrous hair and perfect creamy skin, with only the very beginnings of wrinkles. Having such a beautiful mother was sometimes maddening.

Since I didn't answer immediately—as I wasn't sure what was safe to say—my mom walked over to me and felt my forehead. Once she was satisfied that I wasn't feverish, she asked, "Dearest, is everything all right?"

My mom sounded normal; my parents always called

me "dearest." Unless they were upset with me, in which case they called me by my full name, the archaic-sounding Ellspeth, which I hated.

"I'm okay, Mom. I just woke up from a strange dream. That's all."

Very, very calmly, she asked, "What was the dream, dearest?"

"Nothing. It was only a dream. I better get ready."

I walked back upstairs to my bedroom, grabbed some clothes, and then headed into the bathroom. I looked at my pale blue eyes in the mirror and brushed out my poker-straight black hair. No matter how weird I felt, no matter how changed I believed myself to be, I still looked like perfectly average Ellie, a regular teenage girl who loved reading and travel; had one really good friend, Ruth; and a new boyfriend, Michael. Yet, as I stared at myself in the mirror, I wondered how I was going to act normal, knowing what I knew. Or what I thought I knew.

Because I woke up remembering that Michael and I were *not* normal. We were anything but normal. Sure, when we met, on that first day of my junior year, it felt special, and not only because I was a junior girl and he was a senior guy. I thought that special feeling meant we were falling in love. Then, within weeks, I learned that we shared extraordinary powers that, even now, seemed incredible.

Michael taught me that we could read others' thoughts by touch, even by blood. And he showed me that we could fly. We didn't know exactly what we were, only that we were together in our ignorance.

Michael and I had traveled to Boston to find out who, or what, we were. We learned that we were the long-awaited return of the Nephilim, the half humans and half angels described in Genesis. The Nephilim were prophesied to come at the end of time, to do what we didn't yet know. And I was the Elect One, whatever that meant. To learn the truth, we'd had to kill Michael's birth father, Ezekiel, who turned out to be not so nice.

Ezekiel. Even thinking about him made certain of his words echo in my head. I heard him tell me that my beautiful parents were two of the original fallen angels mentioned in Genesis. That they were banished to roam the earth forever because they'd dared to mate with humankind and create the new Nephilim race in defiance of God. That they were striving to regain grace and so had sacrificed their immortality and angelic powers to raise me as their daughter—even though I wasn't their birth child—and to protect me until it was time for the end.

If it wasn't all a dream . . . and I still wasn't positive what was real and what was a dream. After all, my mom had made no mention of Boston.

I trudged downstairs, leery of what the school day could bring. "I'm ready to go, Mom."

"Michael's picking you up today, Ellie. Don't you remember?"

"I'm not grounded anymore?"

"No, dearest. Your grounding was over this weekend." She paused and then asked, "Are you sure that you're all right?"

"I'm fine, Mom. I'll just go wait for Michael."

After I offered her a few more assurances, I stood by the front door for Michael. The sky started to drizzle, driving out all hopes of that crisp fall day I'd hoped for. Before I had the chance to lament the changeable weather too much—or address any of the troubling questions rumbling about in my head—I heard the crunch of car tires on gravel. My heart started racing in excitement and apprehension. Michael was here. What would I say to him?

After yelling out a final good-bye to my mom, I closed the front door behind me and walked toward his waiting car. He opened the car door for me from the inside, and I slid into his Prius. Finally, after buying myself a few seconds to compose myself by brushing the rainwater off my jacket and organizing my bag, I steeled myself and looked his way.

"How was your night?" he asked in his low, gravelly

voice. No matter how many times I heard it, I always felt like melting. He leaned over to give me a kiss on the cheek.

"Fine," I answered cautiously. "Yours?"

We made small talk about homework assignments, and I glanced over at him again. For the millionth time, I was struck by his looks. He wasn't traditionally handsome. His hair was too blond and his eyes were too light a shade of green for that, although I thought that his tawny skin and tall, leanly muscular body made the combination arresting.

It was his smile that drew me in. I adored the way it brightened his otherwise serious face and the way it made his eyes crinkle. Most of all, I loved how his smile cut right through my attempts at a steely exterior. When he smiled at me, I knew he really saw *me*. Like no one else had done before.

Briefly, I smiled back at him, and in that moment, it didn't matter whether the memories of Boston and our powers and our role in the end days were true. All that mattered was that we were together.

The tranquil moment didn't last. Michael started the car, and "Cemeteries of London," a Coldplay song, came on. He knew it was one of my favorites.

Over the song, he said, "Feels like London out today, doesn't it?"

I froze. Had he said what I thought he had? We had

been heading to London from Boston. Or was Michael's reference to London a coincidence, simply explained by the song?

"So . . . ?" I dared to ask.

As he watched my expression, his smile softened knowingly. And I knew, with utter certainty, that Boston had not been a dream. All those memories were real. And more.

THREE

Excitement coursed through me. Over the certainty that Boston was not a dream. Over the knowledge that my memories of Michael and the flying and the blood were real. Over the realization that, in Boston, we had finally learned who—and what—we were.

But then, as quietly as he could over the music, Michael said, "Ignorance is the only thing that has protected you so far." His words reminded me that the news wasn't all good. There were strings.

Michael and I were *meant* to forget the truth about who we were and what we were destined to do. Because, once we fully grasped that we were indeed the long-awaited Nephilim, the end of time countdown would begin. That knowledge and the full blossoming of our powers would make us irresistible to the fallen angels, and we would become the focus of their end-days game. To prevent the starting of the end-days clock, our parents had shielded us from birth about our real identities. As we started to uncover some truths about our natures and our identities in Boston, they tried to make us forget again with the help of angelic friends who retained their otherworldly powers.

His words unleashed another memory, one that happened *after* we had returned to Tillinghast from Boston but before I'd woken up that morning. I recalled seeing my parents hand in hand, standing before a blond girl of indeterminate age. I was in the room with them, witnessing the whole exchange through some miasma, almost as though I were half asleep.

"Tamiel," my dad said to the girl, "are you certain this will work? She will forget?"

"As certain as I can be of anything right now, Daniel," the girl answered him. "You and Hananel must play your parts as well. You must cast a veil of normalcy over yourselves and all your dealings with her, so that Ellspeth will find it difficult to think of herself as anything other than a typical teenage girl."

My parents had failed. I knew that I wasn't a typical teenage girl. And Michael's parents had failed at the same task too.

I opened my mouth, a hundred questions on the tip of my tongue, but Michael put a quieting finger over my lips. I didn't understand. Why couldn't we talk about this in the privacy of his car? The grave look on Michael's face stopped any protest I considered. Instead, I was left to my own thoughts as we drove to school.

Fear overtook the initial excitement.

It was all too much. It couldn't be true. I was just Ellie Faneuil. I was *not* some legendary biblical creature upon whom the fate of the world hinged. These thoughts kept running through my head over and over again.

I must have looked as sick and frightened and besieged as I felt, because Michael pulled the car off the road and wrapped me in his arms. He pulled me tight against his chest. I felt his heart beating fast and his chest rising, and I realized that he was as terrified as I was.

"It's going to be okay, Ellie. I promise," he whispered into my ear.

I wanted to ask him *how*. How everything was going to be all right, when my entire universe had been turned upside down.

But I couldn't.

Michael pushed back my long black hair from my face, twisting a strand in his fingers. He looked into my blue eyes, as pale as his own. His expression told me that he didn't have any answers either. Only that he loved me.

With his full lips, he kissed me. Hard and long and deep. I could feel his breath mingle with mine, and taste his tongue on my own. With this exchange came the force of our memories, the good memories, that is. Of the long hours we had spent flying the night skies in sheer delight, of the too-short evenings we had passed entwined in each others' bodies, and of the times we had tasted each others' blood through our kisses.

I wanted more. More of Michael. His blood. When our relationship first began, and I learned about the power of blood, the very thought of such an exchange repelled me. Until I learned that the slightest taste of blood gave us insights into each other's minds and souls. When we made that exchange, it brought us a powerful intimacy and joy.

Michael felt my need. He probably felt his own need or desire too, but he must have realized that soon neither one of us would be able to turn away from its call. And he must have known that we could not surrender to it. Or risk everything.

"We can't, Ellie," Michael said as he gently pushed me away.

"Why not?" My hunger for him was so great that I didn't care if I sounded desperate.

"It isn't that I don't want to."

"Then what, Michael?"

Michael didn't answer. Instead, he waited for my breathing to slow, and then he slid a piece of paper onto my lap.

I reached for it. I unfolded the paper, and I recognized
Michael's scrawling script. Why was he writing to me?
Why couldn't he tell me what he needed to say? I wanted to
talk to him, not read some scribbled note.

My Ellie—

Michael knew I loved it when he called me that.
It softened me enough for any message, good or bad.
Undoubtedly, this was his intention.

*We now know who we are. The Nephilim. Half human,
half angel, destined to play some important role at the end.
Whatever that is.*

*Please remember what I overheard our parents say.
Ignorance is the only thing that has protected us so far.
Ignorance about who we are has protected us—protected
everyone, really—from the start of the end-days clock. And,
if Ezekiel is to be believed, that ignorance is the only thing
that has protected our parents from being very mortal pawns
in a deadly game. Our parents have tried to re-create that
ignorance artificially, by using other fallen angels to exercise
their powers of forgetting on us.*

*So we must seem to forget. We must pretend that we are
simply Ellspeth Faneuil and Michael Chase, two normal*

teenagers from Tillinghast. We must make believe in front of our classmates and friends, our teachers and coaches, and especially our parents. Since we can't be certain if the exercise of our powers would lead the fallen angels to believe we have full knowledge of ourselves as Nephilim, we cannot fly or read thoughts or taste blood. We can't take the chance that the use of our powers would trigger the end days and alert the fallen to our whereabouts.

We must even be cautious of speaking aloud the truth to each other. Because, if anyone is watching or listening or tracking us by whatever worldly means they have available to them, they will know.

So until we are ready—until we figure out what we're meant to do and how to do it—we have to play at being wholly human. Until then, only through written words can we fly and taste and truly love. And I do truly love you.

Michael

FOUR

Stepping into the hallways of Tillinghast High School was actually weirder than acknowledging that I was an otherworldly creature.

I watched as girls chatted about their lip gloss, and guys shared apps on their iPhones. I noticed friends giggling about other friends' outfits and teammates thumping each other on the back for games well played. I walked past kids furiously copying their friends' homework assignments and others fumbling with the towers of books in their lockers. Of course, I suffered the occasional "accidental" bump by students still angry with me for the now-infamous Facebook incident in which I took the fall for a nasty prank concocted by two of the more popular junior girls, Piper and Missy, in order to protect many of my fellow students.

I couldn't stop from staring at my classmates in amazement, like they were exotic creatures in the zoo. They had no idea that some kind of Armageddon was heading their way and that I was selected to play a special role at the end. Maybe even stop it. They were oblivious to the fact that all their gossiping and studying and worrying were meaningless.

I felt the simultaneous urge to sob and giggle. The whole notion of Ellspeth Faneuil as savior to the world was both overwhelming and ridiculous.

The only thing keeping me sane while I walked down the hallway was Michael. The link of his fingers in mine was like a tether to our new reality. I believed I could navigate through our conflicting worlds—the frivolous Tillinghast High School and the looming otherworldly battle—with him beside me.

Once I said good-bye to Michael before heading into English class, I lost my anchor. I felt like I'd been cast adrift into an unreal sea.

English class brought me near the brink. The minute I entered the classroom, Miss Taunton launched into me. Like a hawk circling a wounded animal, she bombarded me with questions about our latest assigned novel, which I could barely remember amid the more vivid recollections of my days in Boston and my encounter with Ezekiel. I wanted to scream at her that none of this mattered, even though I didn't dare.

The second that Miss Taunton lay off me, my best

friend Ruth texted me: "Wait for me in the hall after class." Normally, I'd welcome a quick chat with my oldest and best friend in the world, especially if it involved commiseration over Miss Taunton's unfair but not unusual treatment of me. For reasons best known only to herself, Miss Taunton had taken a decided dislike to me. But I didn't know if I could handle a one-on-one conversation with Ruth yet. I had no idea what she remembered. The last time we were together—minutes before I boarded the train to Boston— she had confessed to having seen me fly. Had my parents tried to erase Ruth's memory too, with more success? If so, could I pull off the regular Ellie act? How should I handle Ruth? I pled illness and intermittently coughed throughout class to support my ruse.

At the ringing of the bell, I raced out of class. My head was spinning. I needed a reprieve from the dual universes. A moment to catch my breath, to reassemble myself.

Instead, I ran smack into Piper, my next-door neighbor. She had been ignoring me for weeks, since I decided to take the blame for that wicked Facebook prank. Unbelievably, she had decided that this was the moment to break the silence.

"I know what you did, Ellie. I don't get *why* you did it. Why would you take the blame for something you didn't do? Why would you sit through weeks of detention and being grounded and walk down the hallways, knowing that all the kids in school hate you, and not ever point a finger at me or Missy? I bet you think you're some kind of a saint," she said with a shake of her perfect hair. Yet beneath the part of popular girl that she played so well, I saw the other, secretly self-doubting Piper. And she was pleading for my understanding, even for forgiveness.

I didn't know what to say. Part of me wanted to tell her the truth—that her snide little guess wasn't totally off the mark. I was half angel, and I simply couldn't have sat by and let others suffer at her hand. That she better rethink her future actions and ask absolution for those past, because there wasn't much time left for malevolent games.

The conversation nearly delivered me to the edge. Who was I meant to be? How was I supposed to behave?

Before I could say anything I'd regret, Michael appeared at my side and dragged me away.

"Are you all right, Ellie? You look pale," he said, once we were alone. I must have looked shaken, because alarm registered on his face.

"I'm not sure if I can do this, Michael. I know we need to pretend, but I'm already having a hard time—knowing what we know," I whispered.

He put his arm around my shoulder and walked me down the hallway, bringing us into a darkened alcove.

More than anything, I wanted to stay in that warm, shad-owy recess, wrapped in his arms. It was the only place I felt safe. It was the only place that made sense.

Michael placed his finger under my chin, and tipped my face to his. "Ellie, I know you can."

He slipped another letter into my hands. He nodded that I should read it immediately, so I smoothed out the paper and started.

My Ellie—

Do you remember the first time we went flying over our field? You were so nervous about everything. You were afraid to fall from such heights; you didn't want to embarrass yourself in front of me; you were fearful of doing something so clearly otherworldly. Still, you were determined and strong. And I watched in awe as you furrowed your beautiful brow, willed your fears away, and took to the air.

You were breathtaking up there. The wind at your back, your black hair whipping all around you, you owned the skies. From the beginning.

And the very next day, you walked down the hallways of Tillinghast High School like nothing had happened. Like you were a regular girl—prettier and smarter than all the rest, of course, but just a regular human girl.

You can do that again, Ellie. You can walk the tightrope

between the two worlds with courage and determination.
You've done it before.

I love you,
Michael

I smiled as I read the letter. Somehow he had anticipated my feelings and perfectly knew how to restore my confidence. How to bring me back to myself. Michael truly was my soul mate.

"Thank you," I whispered.

"Remember who you are. Remember that you walked this walk before, and you can do it again."

I nodded and closed my eyes for a second. Conjuring those days from earlier in the fall, my self-assurance returned, slowly and shakily and only on the surface. I had no other option. I *had* to successfully playact at being a regular high school junior, concerned about homework and my new boyfriend. Michael *had* to convincingly make believe that he was an average senior guy, focused on football and college prospects and me. Too much depended on our role-playing.

Off to calculus I went. As I listened to Mr. Dalsimer rattle off theorems, I stopped fixating on the surreal nature of my situation and started to map out my next steps. Focusing on action helped take my mind off my still-shaky core.

By the time class ended, and I joined Michael in the hall-way, I wasn't surprised that his next letter had the same focus. I had already drafted a similar note in my head.

My Ellie—

Now that your resolve has returned, did you spend all of calculus thinking about what we should do next? I bet you didn't take a single note. I'm guessing that you stared out the window, dreaming up a strategy.

I did the same thing.

What should we do next? The trip to Boston definitely gave us a better sense of our natures as Nephilim, and the encounter with Ezekiel linked our births to the emergence of some kind of apocalypse. Crazy as that sounds. We need much more information in order to act next. We need to know exactly what the Nephilim are and were—creation, history, powers, even mortality—and we need to know how the Nephilim fit into this whole end-of-the-world scenario that Ezekiel revealed to us. How are we going to get that knowledge while playing dumb and suppressing our powers? Wouldn't any research we undertook—either in a library or by talking to experts like that professor in London we were going to track down—serve as a red flag to our parents or anyone else who might be seeking us? Wouldn't that be the same as using our powers? Wouldn't it make the fallen aware

*of our knowledge and start the end-days clock ticking? We
need to act, but what do we do?*

*My brilliant, brilliant Ellie. Did you drum up any amaz-
ing ideas in calculus? We need a plan. Now.*

I love you,
Michael

Between the last few periods of the days, we exchanged
a flurry of letters. We each had our theories on how best
to get the information we required, and they weren't the
same. Among other ideas, I proposed that I undertake some
covert research in the university library, under the auspices
of visiting my parents at the office. Michael objected; he
was adamant that I not do any work directly. Instead, he
suggested that, through an intermediary, we reach out to
the professor in London that we had intended to visit after
our trip to Boston. I reminded Michael that Ezekiel knew
about the London professor. Who was to say that Ezekiel
hadn't alerted some of the other fallen that we might try to
contact the professor?

Finally, by the end of the school day, we concocted a
plan we could both agree upon. It was risky. And it was our
only choice.

FIVE

When the last bell rang, I walked Michael over to the football field for his practice, as I would any other day. We needed to stick closely to our usual activities and schedule. Just in case any of the fallen was watching and waiting to see what we knew.

Before he headed into the locker room, I leaned in to kiss him, as I always did. Today, instead of the usual "see you later," I heard him whisper, "Good luck."

I needed it.

I walked over to the parking lot to meet Ruth for an after-school coffee. I knew I had to face Ruth sooner or later, so before our final class I texted her that my cough had subsided and I felt up to our regular meeting. It sickened me to lie to her; we'd always told each other everything.

Amid all the cars and all the kids preparing to bolt from school, I didn't spot her at first. Then I caught a glint of her red hair against the backdrop of the gray day. I hustled over to her used, green VW bug, not sure what reaction I'd get. Did she remember seeing me fly, or didn't she? How was I supposed to behave?

"You look *really* ready for a latte," Ruth pronounced, sounding very normal.

"I am *really* ready for one," I said, attempting to match her light tone.

As we got into her car, I thought how pretty she looked under those wire-rimmed glasses. I smiled a bit, thinking about how shocked our classmates had been when Ruth unleashed her inner runway model at the fall dance, only to tuck that beauty away again for school on Monday. Loyal, whip smart, yet incredibly reserved, Ruth loathed any unnecessary attention. She saved up her animation and lovely smiles for a select few, and most of Tillinghast High School didn't make that cut. I hoped that the frank conversation I planned for our after-school coffee wouldn't wipe the pretty grin right off her face.

I tried to mask my nervousness as we rode to the Daily Grind, and bolstered my courage by remembering the words of Michael's first letter that day. We chatted away, mostly about a benign argument she had had with her new boyfriend, Jamie, about his chronic lateness. The conversation continued as we ordered our coffees and settled into two brown club chairs that sat side by side. As I feigned interest, I lifted my latte to my mouth for a sip. Suddenly, I noticed that my hand was shaking. I put the cup down on the table; I didn't want Ruth to see and wonder why. Not quite yet, anyway.

Once she finished, I waited until the Daily Grind buzzed with noise. Then I scanned the room to make sure no one was paying us the slightest attention. Leaning over the arm of my chair, I slipped a piece of paper into her lap.

I prayed that the information we divulged within wouldn't shatter her world. More fervently, I prayed that after she read the letter, she wouldn't decide Michael and I were crazy and alert my parents to the disclosure, in an effort to "help" us with our delusions, of course. That would undermine everything that Michael and I were trying to accomplish.

Either way, it was a gamble we had to take.

Ruth stared down at the letter sitting in her lap, and said, "What's this?"

"Read it, Ruth. Please."

Laughing, she said, "So we're passing notes now? What are we, in the third grade?"

I bit my lip and motioned for her to read the letter that Michael and I had so painstakingly crafted. I thought about the words we had carefully selected to describe our natures, so as not to upset her too much. We used vague phrases like "special, angelic gifts" instead of describing our ability to fly or, worse, the power of blood. I considered the language Michael and I had used in begging Ruth to help us better understand who we were and what the end days were. We had written about the "mystery of Nephilim selves" and the "looming troubles." And I deliberated on the way we'd explained our inability to do the research ourselves—that others might be watching us and the importance of our pretending to be normal. In the letter, we told her everything we knew . . . but with kid gloves.

Hesitantly, she picked up the letter and unfolded it. I held my breath as she started reading. Even though Ruth had been my best friend for nearly ten years, I didn't know how she would respond to our plea for help researching the nature of the Nephilim and the impending apocalypse. Even though we'd been careful not to use "apocalypse," Ruth was no dummy. How could I possibly predict her reaction to the claim that I was an angel of some sort, no matter how prettily phrased? That our world teetered on the edge of annihilation?

Ruth cleared her throat, and whispered, "So you *do* remember?"

I was flabbergasted. Nothing in her behavior had given me the slightest hint that she remembered anything. "You do too?"

Ruth leaned toward me. In a voice so low that I could barely hear it, she said, "I remember watching you and

Michael fly. And I remember taking you to the train station a few days ago. Today is the first day I've seen you since. I've been so worried about you and Michael, but who could I ask? Certainly not your parents."

Relief coursed through me. I reached over to hug her, and said, "Thank God."

As my hands touched her back and shoulders, I received an intense flash. I saw Ruth pacing her tiny bedroom. Her eyes were red rimmed, and she was staring down at her phone. Desperate with worry over my and Michael's disappearance, she was willing it to ring.

For this very reason, I'd avoided touching anyone since I returned from Boston. Once I made contact with someone, I couldn't prevent *this* exercise of my powers, no matter how hard I tried.

Unaware of the images I'd received, Ruth squeezed me back and whispered, "I thought you had forgotten what you could do, or that I knew about your and Michael's . . . abilities. Or that you didn't want to talk about it for some reason. So when you pretended you were sick earlier today, I kind of backed away from you."

"Now you know why I haven't mentioned it." I tried to apologize. In our letter, Michael and I divulged how our parents had tried to make us forget. And why. To help us, Ruth needed to know everything.

I felt her nod against my shoulder.

"So you'll help us?" I whispered.

"Yes, Ellie. I'll do the research that you and Michael need."

"You understand that there are risks? Huge risks? We don't know if we're being watched. If we are, that means they might start watching you. And we have no idea what else they might do . . . to us or to you!" My voice cracked at even the thought of harm coming to Ruth.

"Of course. That seems very clear." Even though her voice sounded firm and strong, I wondered if she comprehended the dangers. How could she, unless she'd stared evil in the face, as Michael and I had?

I started to cry. "Thank you, Ruth. Thank you so much for helping me and Michael."

"Ellie, I'd do anything for you, you know that. This research, though, you understand that I'm not doing it for you and Michael alone, right?"

"No?"

"I am doing this for everyone, Ellie. Because if I understand your letter correctly, everyone is at risk. If it becomes known that you and Michael understand who you are and what you're meant to do, then you will be engaged in some kind of conflict. And the entire world will hang in the balance."

Six

Michael and I waited. We hung around, wishing that Ruth had some news to share. The rest of the school week, the waiting felt interminable. Here we were, armed with the knowledge that we were elect creatures critical to preventing the impending apocalypse, and we could do *nothing*. Nothing but spend our days suppressing our powers and roaming the halls of Tillinghast High School and the streets of our little town as if we were like the other kids. Nothing but spend our nights attempting to sleep in our beds, while succumbing to increasingly disturbing dreams, instead of soaring in the nighttime skies.

I was ready. And restless. All the waiting shook my vulnerable interior.

The weekend loomed long before me. When Michael announced that he'd have to go to an extra football practice on an uncharacteristically sunny Saturday morning—the coach had called for one since they didn't have a game

Friday night—I decided to sit in the bleachers and half watch, half do my homework. I found it easier to pass the endless hours of waiting when I was in Michael's presence. Somehow, it soothed.

For the first fifteen minutes or so, I watched Michael and his teammates perform drills, while the sunglass-wearing coaches barked orders from the sidelines. Very quickly, the exercises became pretty routine and pretty boring. So I threw myself into my Spanish homework, finding it surprisingly intriguing compared to what was happening on the field.

I was lost in verb conjugations when I felt a tap on my shoulder. I instinctively jumped.

"Hi, Ellie," a familiar voice said.

It was Ruth. "God almighty, you scared me to death." As she moved to sit down on the bleacher next to me, she looked so contrite that I felt bad for chastising her.

"Sorry, Ellie. I should know better, right?"

"Right," I answered with a sigh of relief, as I scooted over to make more room. "What are you doing at school on a Saturday?"

"Yearbook meeting."

"I should have guessed." Ruth always filled her schedule to the brim, hoping that all her good grades and all her leadership activities would merit a college scholarship when the time came.

"Hey, Jamie and I are going to the movies tonight. We're going to see *The Controversy*. Do you and Michael want to join us?"

I paused for a second. Part of me wanted to scold her for not spending every free minute working on our research. Didn't she understand the stakes? I stopped myself. Ruth was doing us a major favor by undertaking such a risky project; I should be very, very appreciative.

"Oh, I don't know if that's a good idea, Ruth." Michael and I had planned a low-key evening: a movie at my house and takeout. Plus, I didn't know if I could face an evening of playacting with Jamie. Pretending to be normal was harder than I thought. I needed a break from it.

"Come on, Ellie. You're supposed to be an everyday, average teenager, aren't you?"

Ruth had a point. I was reluctant, but I decided to give in. "All right. Thanks for asking us."

The Controversy turned out to be a mainstream thriller. Not the kind of foreign or indie film Ruth and I usually liked, but maybe it was Jamie's turn to pick the movie. All the chase scenes and death threats were too close to our recent adventures in Boston for my taste. Still, it was a relief to check out of my own crazy reality for a while.

Afterward, we headed to the diner to have dessert. Over brownie sundaes and apple crisps, we talked about Miss Taunton and the grueling workload she assigned. We had some serious laughs, imagining what her private life must be like, given her strange proclivity for assigning gothic romance.

"How do you manage all your homework and papers with your football practices?" Jamie asked Michael.

"It's tough with Coach Samuel's schedule. Sometimes I'm up all night," Michael answered, smiling at me. I knew what actually kept him up at night. Or what used to, any way. Coach Samuel had arrived at Tillinghast High School during the summer from a Boston high school, with an incredible reputation and an over-the-top work ethic—for himself and his players.

"Seriously?" Jamie asked. He was kind of in awe of Michael.

"Absolutely. It's worth it, though. I mean, Coach Samuel is turning the Tillinghast team into a contender for the state championship," Michael said proudly. Then, in a smaller, more modest voice, he added, "And he's mentioned that, if I work hard enough, he might even be able to get me a football scholarship."

I was surprised. Michael hadn't said anything to me about a football scholarship. In fact, he hardly used to talk about football at all.

Before I could respond, Ruth interjected. "That's amazing, Michael. I'd love to get a scholarship for *anything*." Michael had hit right onto Ruth's dream.

Jamie reached over and put his arm around her shoulder. "You totally will, Ruth. Look at your four point oh grade average; look at all the clubs you are the president of."

While Jamie and Ruth lost themselves in conversation of how amazing he thought she was and how certain he was she'd secure a scholarship, I linked my hand with Michael's. "You never said a word about this whole football scholarship business."

He smiled sheepishly. "Well, we've had a lot of other things on our plates lately, haven't we?"

Looking into his piercing, pale green eyes, I smiled back and said, "We definitely have."

I almost whispered that we needed to solve the end-days problem before we worried about college, but I paused. This whole acting-normal thing was working well for Michael, as it should be. Why should I rain on his parade, because he was better at acting "normal" than me? Because he could lose himself in football when I couldn't find anything to capture my attention—and act as a salve for my nerves—during our interminable wait?

I told myself that I should be happy for Michael's

happiness, regardless of what happened to his dream of college football in the long run. I swallowed my words, squeezed his hand, and said, "A football scholarship would be awesome, Michael. I'm so proud of you."

We said our good-byes to Ruth and Jamie and hopped into Michael's car. But I felt nowhere near tired.

"Are you ready to go home yet?" Michael asked as he started the car.

The prospect of another long night tossing and turning in bed was unappealing. Especially since, before Boston, Michael and I had spent every night together in a secret survey of the skies and each other's bodies.

"No, it seems kind of early for us, doesn't it?" I answered.

Michael reached for my hand. "Way too early to call it a night. Should we go to our field?"

Why hadn't that occurred to me first? So many of my best memories happened there, after all. And Michael had mentioned it in one of his first letters to me. "Yes, that's perfect."

We didn't talk on the ride there. Instead, I thought about the first time Michael brought me to the field; he had told me that it was the only safe location for me to practice flying. He had been so patient with me, even when I gracelessly tumbled to the ground again and again. And he'd been so gentle with me afterward, as we lay together on the springy grass and studied the stars. It became our special spot, the one place we returned to night after night to be our true selves.

It felt weird going to the field in a car. In the past, we had always flown there. I used to circle the ring of evergreens, swooping in and out of their prickly branches in a game of my own design. Only when Michael arrived did I consent to land on terra firma.

Hand in hand now, we walked through the narrow path in the trees. The needles were sharper than I remembered. Perhaps the field would be different, approached by land. Only a few days had passed since we last visited here, but it seemed forever ago, so much had transpired. When we parted the boughs, there it stood. The perfect circle of our field.

The field never failed to take my breath away with its impossibly gorgeous, natural beauty. Within the evergreens' embrace awaited the softest, most vibrant green grass imaginable. Dotted among its blades were unexpected patches of wildflowers and bushes of heather, despite the increasingly chilly fall weather. The skies above afforded a telescopic, crystal-clear view of the heavens. We didn't love the field for its photo-shoot-ready loveliness or the memories it held. We loved it because it felt like home.

Michael sat down on the soft center of the field, which sat a bit higher than the rest of the ground. He motioned for me to join him, and we lay back in each other's arms. I sighed deeply for the first time since we'd left Boston. We didn't speak. We simply gazed at the stars.

The ground was still soft, and the stars were still bright. Michael's embrace was still enticing and comforting. When I surrendered into his arms in this most comforting of places, I surrendered my facade of strength for a moment too. It seemed that I'd shored myself up fairly well on the outside; yet inside, I was still overwhelmed. All my apprehensions about being the Elect One—fears that I'd worked hard to suppress since we returned from Boston—flooded to the surface. I started to cry, a deep, wracking sob. How on earth was I going to rise to my calling?

Michael's arms tightened around me. "Hey, we're going to get through this. Together."

I tried to calm myself. Despite my efforts, my breaths were halting and shallow. "Do you promise?"

Michael turned to me and looked me directly in the eyes. We stared at each other for a long moment, and I thought for the hundredth time how mesmerizing his pale green eyes were. Especially when they bore the promise of his devotion.

"I promise, Ellie."

He must have seen some hesitation, some modicum of doubt in my eyes, because he drew me even closer to him. "Ellie, I have loved you since I first laid eyes on you. I feel like I have waited my whole life to prove that love to you. Keeping this promise will be that proof."

The strength of his words dried my tears. The length of our bodies touched, and it occurred to me that this was the closest we'd been physically since the car ride we took to school on our initial return from Boston. We had taken care not to be alone too often.

I felt the heave of his chest against mine, and the warmth of his muscled thigh against my own. I felt his breath on my cheek, and his fingers entwined in my hair. And more.

Suddenly, I wanted him. Not his blood. I knew I couldn't have that. Him.

We'd never gone too far before. Physically, that was. Sharing each other's blood always seemed the most intimate, the most complete, of acts. We couldn't do that at the moment, and we both needed something more.

We were just teenagers now. Wasn't this what other teenagers did? Then Michael dragged me on top of him, and the motion drove all thoughts from my mind.

He kissed me hungrily, as if it had been months instead of weeks since we'd been together. I returned his fervor, running my tongue along his full lips and neck. Yet he still felt too far away from me. Despite the cold, I unbuttoned his shirt, and ran my hands up his muscled stomach to his chest. His skin felt silky and warm, almost hot, under my fingers, and the sensation made me want to touch him more.

Emboldened by my actions, Michael fumbled at the buttons on my jacket and then slid his hands under my wool sweater. His hands felt cold and rough and sexy on my skin, and when he reached around to undo my bra, I kissed him even harder.

Shirt undone, hair wild, Michael rolled me under him. I wrapped my legs around his strong thighs, and drew him even closer to me. I could no longer feel the cold night air on my skin, only the warmth of Michael's breath and hands and lips all over my willing body.

We were both panting, and I knew that we'd reached the moment. The moment of no return.

Gently, Michael pulled his face away from mine to look at me with his pale, pale eyes. His eyes brimmed with adoration and desire. I never loved him more than in that moment. And I never wanted him more than in that moment.

Then his face darkened.

"What's wrong?" I asked.

"Ellie, I'm not sure I'll be able to stop."

"I don't want you to," I whispered.

"I mean, I don't know if I'll be able to stop at this."

The blood. Michael didn't think he'd be able to stop with our bodies. He worried that the urge for blood would prevail. We could not allow that to happen. It could be like a beacon for the fallen.

Awkwardly, we sat up. I pulled down my sweater and struggled to rebutton my jacket, while Michael did the same. Mixed emotions plagued me. I was disappointed that Michael had put on the brakes but also a little relieved. I didn't know if I was totally ready to take the leap.

Michael reached over and hugged me tight. "This is the right decision, Ellie, believe me. There will be plenty of time for this. After."

His words saddened me. Would there be time? Or was the end so imminent that this was our only chance to be physically intimate with each other? "I hope so, Michael."

He whispered. "Don't worry. We'll make time for this."

"No, Michael, you misunderstood me. I meant that I hope that there will be an 'after.'"

SEVEN

The indulgent escape of our weekend over, Michael and I were forced to return to the facade of being ordinary students. The endless round of classes; homework; and, for Michael, football practice took our minds off the waiting a bit. Although Michael still seemed better able to escape into the normal-teenager routine. We were afraid, though, that pretending to forget might someday become the same thing as forgetting.

So we promised to keep on writing our letters, especially because we didn't know the potential danger lurking in the exercise of our powers. We couldn't fly anymore, so we experienced the joy and freedom of soaring down the coast through our words. We wouldn't take the risk of actually reading another's thoughts, so instead we described the rush we got off a flash from another mind. We couldn't dare sample each other's blood, so we sought out terms to capture the intense closeness we felt when we used to. We didn't dare become physically intimate, so we wrote words of love to each other instead. Through our letters, Michael and I clung to the truth.

On Monday and Tuesday, the letters sufficed. They even seemed romantic in an old-fashioned, Jane Austen sort of way. Michael always had a note waiting for me in his hand when we met up after every class, and I had one for him. I couldn't wait to get to the next class, where I could unfold the pages slowly and secretly and lose myself in his words. For a few glorious minutes, I'd return to the nights earlier in the fall when Michael and I were free to revel in our powers and each other, before we learned too much about why we had our powers. His phrases got me through the endless school days and strengthened my resolve that we would make it through to the other side of the end days, whatever that meant.

Yet, on Wednesday, Michael didn't have a letter prepared for me after English class. It was the very first time this had happened since our return from Boston. Tuesday night's grueling football practice, he explained apologetically, had left him so spent that he fell asleep during first period. Even though I was disappointed, I understood, of course; Coach Samuel had been running him ragged, even giving Michael extra workouts because he thought he had the talent to play college football. Michael tried to make it up to me by having notes at the ready after the rest of my classes. And I relished them, even though they were somewhat shorter than the ones I'd grown accustomed to.

For some reason, when I got home after school on Wednesday, rebellious thoughts wormed their way into my consciousness. Starting with my parents. As I sat across the dinner table from them, pretending everything was hunky-dory, certain of Ezekiel's claims nagged at me. He had told me that my parents weren't my birth parents, that they had adopted me. That my human mother had died. As I passed the salt or answered my parents' inane questions about homework, I felt myself get angry at them for keeping the truth from me, even if they thought they were doing it for the right reasons.

I found myself wondering about my biological parents. Who were they? Tamiel had confessed that my human mother was "gone," but would say no more. Did she mean dead? And where was my father? Since he must be a fallen angel—an immortal—he must be roaming the earth somewhere. I couldn't ask my parents any of these questions, or reveal everything Michael and I had worked to hide. Instead, the questions seethed beneath the surface, making me angrier and angrier at all this pretending.

Nighttime offered little relief from the disloyal churning of my mind. I tossed and turned in my bed, thinking about how Michael treated me before I left for Boston. I relived the evening when he lured me to Ransom Beach with promises of watching the sunset together. I experienced again the feeling of betrayal when Michael instead foisted Ezekiel upon me and—right before my eyes—became an automaton for Ezekiel's commands to sway me toward his sick quest for power. Telling myself that the Ransom Beach Michael wasn't *my* Michael but some zombielike Ezekiel follower only went so far.

When I was finally able to drift off to sleep, the dreams came. Unsettling visions of death and destruction. The images reminded me of the horrific flashes I'd received from Ezekiel's mind. Except for one, in which a luminous sword vanquished the darkness.

When I awoke on Thursday morning, I wondered what was happening to me. Why was I harboring these unfaithful thoughts about my parents and, more disconcertingly, Michael? Was my self-doubt over being the Elect One running rampant and taking Michael as its target? Michael was my love, my soul mate, the one who always had my back. I mean, he had even killed his own father to protect me.

Did these subconscious doubts actually stem from the change in the frequency and length of Michael's notes? Why should it matter if his letters were shorter? Or if he skipped sending a letter after a class or two? It seemed ridiculous, especially in the context of the looming end days. Did I have misgivings because Michael had thrown himself into football? If so, that was totally unfair of me, since we had agreed to act as normally as possible. And for Michael, football was normal.

Since I didn't have an answer, I chalked it up to the strain of waiting for the results of Ruth's research. Or, I thought, maybe it stemmed from the fact that anything *real* Michael and I needed to say had to be committed to paper. It was taking a toll, yet I couldn't afford to entertain personal problems.

I needed to shake off my doubts. I needed to stay focused. I reminded myself that I was strong. I was a Nephilim. I was the Elect One.

So, on Thursday evening, I decided to throw myself into a paper on Edith Wharton for the odious Miss Taunton instead of brooding. Since pretending was the name of the game these days, I had decided to knock Miss Taunton's socks off with my brilliance. More important, her challenging assignment took my mind off *everything.* Even the crumpled-up note from Michael on my nightstand, the one he'd ended abruptly—with a "see you later" instead of "love"—because he had to run to practice.

The phone rang. I heard it, but I was too deeply engrossed in *The Age of Innocence* to have it truly register.

"Dearest, it's Ruth," my mom yelled up the stairs.

Why hadn't Ruth called me on my cell? She knew I kept it on my desk when I was doing homework. As I picked up the phone, I took a quick look at my cell, and realized that it was my fault; I'd inadvertently turned the ringer off. Even still, between my big-picture problems, my minor frustrations over English, and my lack of sleep, I was feeling uncharacteristically irritable.

I picked up the phone, guessing at why she'd be calling. "Hey, Ruth. If you're calling for some tips about writing this stupid English paper, don't bother. I have no insights to offer. I'm struggling myself." Even though I was committed to the assignment, I couldn't help my irritation at having to deliver on my English homework. I mean, would mastery of the finer details of Edith Wharton's life help in the apocalypse?

"I wouldn't worry about the paper too much, Ellie."

"Why? You don't think that Miss Taunton is going to give us some slack, do you? I wouldn't bet on it."

"No, Ellie, that's not why."

"Then why?"

"I think it'd be better if we talked it over in person. Can you meet me at the coffee shop tonight?"

"No, Ruth. It's almost nine. I don't think my parents would be too thrilled about me going to the Daily Grind right now. Plus, I have to finish this paper by tomorrow morning. And so do you."

Her patience finally ran out, turning her sweet tone sour. "Ellie, I think you have more important things to worry about than Miss Taunton's paper. In fact, that paper is the least of your problems."

I felt sick to my stomach. I suddenly had a feeling where this conversation was going. "What do you mean?"

"All this pretending that you and Michael have been doing isn't working. The end days have already begun."

Eight

I convinced my parents to let me go to the Daily Grind. I told them that Ruth was upset about a fight with Jamie and needed consoling. They were reluctant. Still, they agreed on the condition that I only stay an hour.

I don't know what excuse Michael offered his parents, but he made it there too, after I called him. Even though he greeted me with his usual kiss, he seemed distracted. It was almost like we'd interrupted him from something *really* important. What could be more critical than preventing the end of time?

The Daily Grind was surprisingly busy, given the hour. The high school crowd apparently moved out around seven P.M., only to be replaced by the college students later on. Even though no one said it aloud, I knew we were all thankful for the bustle around us. It softened the tension. It made us all feel less alone.

We managed to secure a table from a group of departing

students. After we took our seats, I reached for Michael's hand while we waited for Ruth to finish rummaging through her bag. He grasped mine back. It made me feel reconnected to him, particularly after the disloyal thoughts I'd harbored the day before.

Ruth cleared her throat and slid a folder to us across the table. She was visibly nervous. At last, she whispered, "I think the earthquakes going on around the world are the first sign of the end days."

"The earthquakes?" Michael asked.

Ruth looked over at Michael in surprise. "You know, the magnitude seven jolt that the Caribbean got several days ago that's causing all sorts of devastation? And the seven and eight magnitude earthquakes that have happened in China, Chile, Japan, Indonesia, and California over the past week? Maybe you haven't heard about those since they're getting much less play in the media."

She could be very literal. At the worst times.

"I've seen the news, Ruth," Michael responded a bit defensively. "I meant, how could the earthquakes be signs? Signs of what?"

"I guess I should back up a couple steps. You guys have heard of the Book of Enoch?"

We both nodded. I had researched it myself at the Andover-Harvard Theological Library in Boston. Ezekiel had quoted from it liberally and ominously. My stomach flipped at the mention of it.

"Okay, then you know that some biblical experts believe that the Book of Enoch describes the emergence of the Nephilim and the Elect One. Some experts theorize that this Elect One will surface as the apocalypse begins. The Elect One is the only being who can stop the end days and save the earth—and all the humans on it—from certain destruction. Or enslavement by the darkness, depending on which expert you're reading."

Ruth continued. "Well, the Bible book that truly gets into the end days is Revelation, one of the most complicated and nonlinear books of the Bible. In Revelation, God hands a scroll to a figure called the Lamb. The Lamb has been interpreted to be a messianic figure, kind of like the Elect One. This scroll has seven wax seals, each of which represents the seven events or signs that will happen before the annihilation of the earth. Revelation also mentioned seven trumpets—seven other events—that could happen after the seven seals. Since most experts don't focus on the seven trumpets, I didn't either. I stuck to the seven seals. Simplified and in this order, the seven seals are the following: earthquakes; famine; widespread disease; economic depression; persecution of Christians; warfare; and the emergence of a leader who will seem to unite people in the face of all this devastation but who actually has other, more nefarious plans. This leader has been described as a sort of anti-Messiah. Once this leader comes on the scene with the seventh seal, well, Revelation lists all kinds of terrible events he or she will inflict on the earth to bring about the end. In order to stop the earth's destruction, either the Lamb or the Elect One—must stop these seven seals."

Ruth took a deep breath before speaking again. "I've been studying the news and looking for patterns. I wanted to see if all this pretending to be normal that you two are doing is stopping the clock of these end days events. I'm pretty sure your pretending has failed."

I felt sick to my stomach. "What do you mean?"

"I think the earthquakes are the first sign."

Michael pulled his hand away from mine and said, "There have been hundreds of earthquakes in the past. And they didn't signal the end of time."

Ruth motioned for us to open the folder. Inside, I found newspaper articles and charts and graphs and summaries of current and past world events. When Ruth took on a task, she really took it on.

"At no other point in history have there been earthquakes quite like this, not as many of this magnitude in such a short time, anyway. It seems that the earth is in an especially volatile phase." She paused. "And it seems that the earth entered this phase precisely when you and Ellie learned who you were."

Michael was momentarily silenced.

"Could it be a coincidence?" I asked, pleading for the impossible.

"I don't think so, Ellie." Ruth reached out and touched my empty hand. "I'm so sorry. I think the clock started the moment you learned the truth. Never mind that your parents tried to make you forget and never mind all your pretending."

Michael interjected, "This can't be right. I understood what Ezekiel said. I knew that it might be coming. That said, this couldn't possibly be the beginning of the end days. I mean, look around at all these kids getting their coffee and going about their daily business. Would the apocalypse look like this?"

I heard the fear in his voice. We hadn't liked the waiting. Right now, it seemed preferable to this next, terrifying stage of knowledge. We should've been more careful what we wished for.

Since I clearly didn't have the heart to reproach him, Ruth took on the job of admonishing him instead. "Michael, you asked me to research the Nephilim and the end days, and I did. I can't help it if you don't like what I found. Or if you don't believe it."

Michael's face softened, and I saw remorse in his eyes. "I'm sorry, Ruth. You're right. The news is hard to take, that's all. Don't kill the messenger, right?"

Ruth managed a forgiving chuckle.

Michael reached for my hand again. The warmth of his hand in mine offered some comfort. It reminded me that I was not alone in all this madness.

"What does your research say that Ellie and I should do next?" He asked the logical next question. One I should have asked myself, but all this talk of the Elect One was clouding my thinking.

"Boiled way down, Revelation says that the Elect One has to stop the signs to stop the apocalypse. Unfortunately, it definitely doesn't offer any step-by-step instructions as to how the Elect One should go about that. It's no how-to guidebook, that's for sure. Revelation is far too dense and cryptic for that; it's written with all this crazy symbolic imagery. I thought our best bet would be to try and predict the next sign. And then evaluate what you guys could do to prevent it from happening."

"I'm guessing that you've already started that little project?" I asked with a smile. If I knew Ruth, she'd probably already created bar graphs and statistical models forecasting the next sign.

Ruth smiled. "Of course." Her smiled faded, as she

added, "I don't have anything definitive at the moment."

"So we wait some more," Michael said with a heavy sigh.

Ruth nodded apologetically. "We wait. Not too long, though. I don't think we have too long."

I asked, "Should we tell our parents? They might be able to give us some answers. You know, they were angels at one point. And it sounds like our playacting hasn't stopped the end days anyway."

"Even though our pretending to forget might not be preventing the end days, it still might be offering them some protection, Ellie," Michael answered quietly. "I hope so, anyway."

I thought back to Ezekiel's warning that we could bring harm upon our parents if we told them what we knew. Maybe Ezekiel's words carried an empty threat, but we couldn't take the chance. My parents were mortal now, after all, and I didn't think they had any angelic means left to protect themselves against the likes of Ezekiel or his fallen kin.

"We keep them in the dark, for now," I agreed.

"For now."

My cell phone beeped. I looked down and saw a "gentle reminder" text from my parents. I picked up my bag and said, "Well, I better get home. My hour is up."

Michael stood up as well. "I better go too. I have a game tomorrow night."

How could he think of a football game at a time like this? I almost said something but stopped myself. Maybe Michael was simply playing the part of dedicated football player. Much like I had adopted the role of keen English student. I shouldn't judge him. We had committed ourselves to the playacting. For now.

NINE

In the spirit of our playacting, I made plans with Ruth to watch Michael's football game. As his girlfriend, I had always loyally attended his games, even though I wasn't much of a sports fan. Michael and I figured we should stick to our usual pattern.

Like many of our classmates, Ruth and I hung around the school library, doing homework and chatting, before the game began. No one wanted to leave campus and chance losing their spot in the school parking lot. The Tillinghast football team was so excellent that it had developed a following way beyond the high school students. Plus, it was better for me to stay away from home. I was afraid that, if I spent too much time with my parents, I'd spill everything or get angry with them over the whole birth parents thing. The school library was definitely the safer option.

Ruth and I left the library early to secure a good seat, and it turned out to be a smart move on our parts. Even though the game wasn't scheduled to start for nearly an hour, the bleachers were beginning to fill up with students, parents, and townspeople alike. Even so, we managed to nab a spot with a clear view of the field and the sidelines. While I enjoyed watching Michael's athletic prowess on the field, I loved studying his face after he finished a play, when he thought no one was paying him any attention.

By the time Ruth and I finished our popcorn and drinks—our pathetic substitute for dinner—the stands were full to capacity, and the crowds were ready. I felt the anticipation building in the fans, and found myself getting swept up in their excitement. When Michael ran out onto the field with the rest of the team, I was on my feet right alongside them, cheering loudly.

He looked amazing out there in our school's navy and white football uniform. It showed off his broad shoulders and sculpted arms and legs, although I was the only one who knew the strength and power contained within his body. Michael literally took my breath away.

I stared as Michael slowed his pace and took his place on the sidelines. An assistant coach came over to his side with a few instructions, and Michael nodded in agreement. Although the helmet hid a large part of his face, I studied him as he waited anxiously for the game to begin. Somehow, he must have sensed my eyes upon him, because he turned to me and smiled.

For a moment, it was only the two of us. No crowds, no announcements, no music. Just Michael and Ellie.

The whistle sounded, shattering our little moment. The next two and a half hours flew by. Even if I tried, I couldn't have articulated the details of the Tillinghast team's victories—or Michael's feats, of which there were many. I became so swept up in the roar of the crowd and the delirium of the triumph that it felt like the game had fast-forwarded right to its successful conclusion.

As soon as the game ended and the players gathered to run off the field together, I felt a compulsion to be with Michael. I couldn't stop thinking about how amazing he looked on the field.

"I'm heading down to the field, Ruth," I called to her over the din.

"Come on, Ellie. You're not going to brave all that," she yelled back in disbelief, gesturing to the jam-packed bleachers and aisles.

"I need to see him."

"Why don't you wait until afterward? Like a normal girlfriend," she said, taunting me a bit.

I shook my head; waiting wouldn't do. I couldn't delay hugging him and telling him how proud I was. Maybe it was my small way of making up to him for all my secret, disloyal thoughts. Who knew? Regardless, Ruth knew better than to argue once my mind was set, so she shrugged in response. Off I went.

The crowd looked a lot worse than it actually was. Pretty quickly, I made my way onto the field and toward the only entrance to the locker room. Coach Samuel, easily identifiable because he wore his usual Tillinghast baseball cap, was talking to a bunch of local reporters near the door, and most of the team congregated nearby. Michael stood next to his teammates.

But he wasn't alone. Three very pretty junior girls, Missy among them, gathered around him. One girl was giggling too hard at something Michael had said, while another clutched at his bicep. And he was laughing along with them, reveling in all the attention.

I froze. The sight of him being fawned over sickened me. Particularly by the golden blond, nasty Missy, whose actions had caused so many so much pain. It made me feel like the old, awkward Ellie I'd been before I met Michael. Instinctively, I pivoted and headed back onto the field.

I'd almost made it across the field, back toward the bleachers, when I felt a hand on my arm.

"Ellie, where are you going?" It was Michael.

I kept walking. "I couldn't stand around and watch those girls throw themselves at the football hero Michael Chase."

Michael turned me toward him. His fair hair was dark with sweat, and his eyes appeared greener against the black smears beneath them. Most of all, he looked genuinely perplexed.

"Missy and her little friends back there? Flirting with you?" I clarified for him, since he seemed so confused.

"Them? Why would you care about them? You know I don't."

"You seemed to be enjoying yourself." I *hated* the way I sounded. On one level, I knew it was absurd to fret over Michael while the world was ticking toward its end. The fact that my feelings were ridiculous didn't stop me from feeling insecure and jealous.

"Ellie, I can't stop those girls from flirting with me. And their flirting means nothing to me." He fixed my gaze. "You know I love only you, don't you?"

Staring right into his serious expression, I nodded. Michael was right. I knew he was right. I was projecting all my self-doubt about being the Elect One onto Michael. I allowed myself to be enfolded in his arms and surrender to the comfort they offered.

TEN

Yet, Michael's arms could not protect me that night. They could not shield me against the terrors of the darkness. Some things I had to face by myself.

Like the dream.

I stood in a dark, cavernous space. The tiled walls bore a damp sheen, and the air smelled wet and moldy. I could hear a slow, steady drip in the background, and it felt like I was in some kind of a subterranean room.

I wasn't alone. Before me was a man. He was not known to me.

He was ruggedly handsome in a blunt, powerful sort of way. His hair was wavy and black. Even though his face was unlined and his hair bore no streak of gray, he seemed older. Yet his age was hard to define, particularly since he knelt before me with downcast eyes.

"Mercy, Ellspeth. I beg you for mercy," the man said, although it didn't sound much like begging to me. His voice sounded strong and confident, like it belonged to someone used to getting his way. "Do you have any mercy in your heart?"

I scoffed at his halfhearted request. "Mercy? Why should I offer you mercy? After all you've done to me. After all the evil you've inflicted upon others."

"Please, Ellspeth, it only seems like evil because you don't understand it. When you are creating a new world, sacrifices must be made. Sacrifices that will eventually yield a greater good." I knew that he meant his tone to soften me. And I could see that he believed in the veracity of his words. Yet I felt no leniency in my heart, only sadness and determination.

"Like my mother? Was she a necessary sacrifice?"

The man raised his gaze from the floor, and looked up at me. For the first time, I realized that his eyes were a startling, pale blue. Like mine.

His eyes filled with resignation and sadness. "I promised your mother that when this moment came, I would surrender to your decision. If you have no mercy to offer, I must accept your merciless sentence," he said quietly, never losing my gaze.

I lifted my arms high above my head. I felt something heavy in my hands, but I didn't know what it was. The room filled with a pure white light, almost like rarefied sunlight. It was the light of judgment.

Then I woke up.

Was the dream a vision of some future event? Was it a remnant of some awful image I'd procured from Ezekiel's mind? Was I simply imagining the birth father that I'd been thinking about so much lately? What made this dream so different from all the rest?

I didn't know. The not knowing made the dream incredibly hard to shake.

Eleven

By the time school rolled around on Monday morning, I was fed up. Fed up with Michael and Ruth always being so preoccupied. Fed up with playacting with everyone around me. Fed up with the disturbing dreams that inundated me every single night. Fed up with the uncertainties that plagued me beneath my self-assured surface. And really, really fed up with waiting, knowing that the end days were upon us.

I needed action. Any kind of action.

As I walked to my locker after the last bell, wondering how to get the action I craved, I noticed a cluster of kids around the main bulletin board. The communal board was covered with advertisements and notices about extracurricular activities and typically didn't warrant too much attention. I usually walked right past it, along with every other student.

I was curious to see what the small crowd was staring

at. As I drew closer, I realized that they were all gathered around a poster announcing the formation of a county-wide committee to raise funds for the earthquake victims. The first meeting was tonight at seven in the school gymnasium.

It seemed the perfect, temporary solution. Normally, I wasn't much of a joiner. Right now I had energy to burn, and I felt partly responsible for all the tragedy. If I'd better understood my role and known how to stop that first sign, then maybe a lot of suffering could have been avoided. Pitching in wouldn't offer much, but it was something.

Then I noticed that Missy stood in the small crowd of kids. And she noticed me. If Missy was planning on joining the committee, maybe I'd reconsider.

"More selfless acts for Ellie, I see," she said, giving me a nasty little grin and a flip of her blond ponytail. I knew—and she knew—that it was a snide reference to the blame I took for her and Piper over the Facebook prank. Her comment was incredibly bold; I guessed she figured that I wasn't planning on turning her and Piper in at this late stage.

"What on earth would draw *you* to a committee that helped people, Missy? I thought your forte was embarrass-ment and humiliation. Until I stopped you, anyway." Tit for tat. If Missy was up for bandying about her malicious deed, so was I. Especially since I didn't see on Missy's face even a shred of the gratitude—or remorse—I'd spotted on Piper's.

"You never know what cute guys might join a committee like that. Like Michael." Her jibe hurt after the little scene I'd interrupted on Friday night, particularly on the heels of a day without any letters from Michael, even though we'd agreed to stop them for now.

"Or your Zeke," I goaded her right back. I was in no mood for turning the other cheek. Missy had picked the wrong day to pick a fight with me.

Missy froze. I could almost see the wheels of her cruel mind turning. How did I know about her mysterious boyfriend, the one who disappeared the night of the fall dance? she wondered. Part of me wanted to tell her what had actually happened to her precious Zeke—really, Ezekiel.

Instead of beating me down, as Missy had intended, our exchange emboldened me. I would definitely go to the committee meeting, to make sure that it met its purpose instead of becoming some big pickup scene. I would make it my outlet for action, for now.

Afterward, I suffered through another dinner with my parents, where I discussed trivialities over pasta primavera while thinking about the impending apocalypse. Hiding a secret this big from my parents was painful, and

I was sure they could sense something was off. Yet they never questioned me.

I asked to borrow the car after dinner, not knowing how they'd respond, given their environmentalist mission to reduce our carbon footprint. To my surprise, they actually agreed. The committee meeting seemed to merit an exception to their stringent rules about walking everywhere, especially when they learned I'd be going alone. Ruth and Michael were too busy with football and schoolwork.

I pulled into the school parking lot a few minutes before seven, figuring I had plenty of time to make it into the gymnasium before the meeting began. But I hadn't banked on the main lot being completely full. I wondered whether there was some kind of a scheduled event that I'd missed hearing about. Usually the cars emptied out of school lot by five, unless there was a Friday football game.

The big clock over the gymnasium doors read seven fifteen by the time I'd parked in a remote lot and run across the campus. Hoping to muffle the gymnasium doors' usual loud creak and sneak into the meeting unnoticed, I opened one of the doors slowly. With no success. The screeching noise announced my entry.

A vast sea of faces turned in my direction. Suddenly, I understood why all those cars were in the lot. Students from all over the county were here to help.

An unfamiliar girl at the podium—presumably the committee organizer—paused when I walked into the room. While she waited for me to sit, she tapped her pencil on the podium and she smoothed her long, light brown hair. I could feel myself blush as I scanned the packed room for an open seat.

The chairs on the floor and the bleachers were nearly at capacity. Among the many unfamiliar kids, I recognized quite a few Tillinghast students. To my astonishment, I even saw Piper and Missy in the crowd. Did Missy have no shame?

Finally, I spied an opening on a bleacher in the far left corner of the room, next to a broad-shouldered guy wearing jeans and a flannel shirt. Scuttling by the rows of chairs and the podium where the organizer resumed her speech, I asked the guy if he could move over to make room for me.

"Like to make a grand entrance, do you?" he whispered with a mischievous smile as he slid over.

I glanced at his face. His hair was chestnut brown and his eyes were dark, almost black. He was handsome in a rough, unfinished sort of way. The flush on my cheeks deepened. They were probably crimson by now. "Sorry about that."

The guy smiled again. In a deep, husky voice, he said, "Don't worry. I was happy for the interruption. The organizer, Amanda, goes to my school, and she likes the sound of her own voice way too much."

I tried to turn my attention to Amanda. But I couldn't. I found myself staring down at the guy's wide, calloused hands and strong thighs. There was something compelling about him, something I couldn't quite describe.

"Told you she drones on," he said, obviously noticing my drifting concentration.

I couldn't suppress a giggle, although it seemed so inappropriate under the circumstances. Here we were on the brink of a major catastrophe—one far worse than most people could possibly comprehend, one in which I was destined to play a major role—and I was giggling at some joke made by a strange guy. I covered my mouth. What on earth was I doing?

He reached over and very lightly touched my hand. As if hearing my thoughts, he said, "It's okay. I'm the only one that heard you laugh."

The exchange so unnerved me that, when Amanda called for volunteers, I just stuck up my hand. I didn't even know what I was volunteering for. The guy next to me raised his arm too.

Amanda pointed to us. "Rafe, you're in. And, you"—she pointed to me—"what's your name?"

"Ellie. My name is Ellie."

"Great, we have two volunteers for the event-planning subcommittee. Anybody else?"

Hands had surfaced throughout the crowd, although I noticed that Piper and Missy lowered their arms as soon as they saw that I'd been selected for the subcommittee. It seemed that Missy didn't mind taunting me for a few minutes in the safety of a crowded hallway but didn't want to spend too much time with me in a small subcommittee meeting. I smiled at the thought of scaring away the indomitable Missy.

As Amanda worked her way around the room, culling volunteers, the guy turned to me. "Since we'll be working together, I guess I should properly introduce myself. I'm Rafe. Rafe Gregory."

He stuck out his hand in greeting.

I almost didn't take Rafe's hand. I'd avoided touching anyone other than Michael or Ruth since I'd returned from Boston, because I didn't want to experience any flashes. Then I thought twice. I'd had a strong reaction to him; and these days, strong reactions unnerved me. Was he really an average high school kid? There was only one way to be certain.

I extended my hand. As we shook, initially I received a very mild flash from him. I saw Rafe as a very small child, maybe three or four, flying a bright red kite. The sky was

unbroken cerulean blue, and young Rafe was delighted
with the way the red stood out against the sky's vivid blue-
ness. I wondered what made him think of that image right
now.

The scene was quickly replaced with a more intense
flash. Through Rafe's eyes, I watched myself entering the
gymnasium. He stared at me as I hunted around for an
empty seat, and I felt his pleasure when I noticed the opening next to him. As I sat down, I heard him thinking how
cute I was.

I quickly withdrew my hand, even though I kind of
liked another guy thinking nice thoughts about me after
watching Michael get so much attention from other girls.
But honestly, I didn't need any more information, because
I had the answer to my question. Yes, Rafe seemed like an
average teenage guy.

Rafe looked at me and smiled. "And you are Ellie—?"

"Ellie Faneuil. I'm Ellie Faneuil."

"Nice to meet you, Ellie Faneuil. Looks like we'll be seeing quite a bit of each other."

TWELVE

The committee had meetings planned for the next two nights. The worldwide need was desperate and urgent, so Amanda proposed that we organize a county-wide party for high-school students in two weeks time. For the first time in days, I felt useful and busy. It quelled the misgivings about my role that lurked beneath my exterior.

On Tuesday and Wednesday nights, the twenty subcommittee members—me, Rafe, two senior girls from Tillinghast I didn't know except by sight, fifteen kids from neighboring high schools, and the prissy, rigid Amanda—spent hours figuring out how to coordinate an enormous event on such short notice. Even though I was certainly not a partygoer, I relished mapping out the tasks, creating a timeline, and making lists of potential donors for drinks, food, decorations, and even music for the party. I liked rolling up my sleeves and *doing* something instead of sitting around my house. All the work took my focus off the end days.

As did watching Rafe and Amanda spar.

"You think that it matters to the earthquake victims if the invitations are printed in blue ink or green?" Rafe was exasperated with Amanda's long monologue on the party invitations' lettering. He didn't have to say it out loud. He clearly thought that Amanda was using the earthquakes as an excuse to host a big party.

"Of course it matters, Rafe. We want as many people to attend the party as possible, don't we?"

"And you truly think the deciding factor will be the invitation ink color? That kids won't come out to help alleviate an enormous tragedy unless they find the invitations aesthetically pleasing?"

"You never know what will sway people's decisions, Rafe," Amanda said primly, as she held up yet another invitation mock-up for the subcommittee to vote upon.

I stifled a laugh as Rafe rolled his eyes in utter frustration at Amanda's perspective. No matter how misguided and myopic they were, she was tenacious in her beliefs. As was he.

"Amanda, we shouldn't be spending our time worrying about invitations or music or decorations. Whatever we end up with will be good enough for the people who come, the ones who genuinely care. Instead, we should be focusing on educating kids about the disaster. So they'll want to help."

While the rest of us listened—even Amanda—Rafe explained that the party was a prime opportunity to reveal what the news reports didn't. He argued that the media was understating the damages. With compassion and persuasion, he spouted off specific data about the number of people killed and injured in each earthquake region and the economic and agricultural harm suffered in those sectors. Data that made the earthquakes seem so much more real, and more deadly, than I'd ever imagined. I knew I needed to hear the information he had at his fingertips, but I didn't like it one bit.

No one spoke after Rafe finished. His message inspired that kind of quiet reverence, as did his delivery. His coarse, challenging exterior masked a thoughtful, surprisingly tender interior. I liked the combination. Especially compared to Michael's current football focus.

Slowly and deliberately, Amanda stood up. Placing her hands on her hips, she said, "Thank you for your lecture, Rafe. If what you say is true, it is important information indeed. However, this is the *party planning* subcommittee. Perhaps your interests would be better suited to another subcommittee. You are welcome to take your talents elsewhere."

Amanda had finally silenced Rafe. I had been wondering the same thing myself. Why had he picked this subcommittee out of all the choices available?

The entire group held their breaths as Rafe made his decision. He glanced over at me for a split second and then said, "I'll stick with this one."

Amanda beamed in victory. "Good, glad to have you. However, given your views, I think I'll take you off the decorations assignment, Rafe. The kids wouldn't want to see some gruesome news photos plastered on the walls that you might deem suitable or educational, while they're at a party. I think I'll put you on the food donations assignment with" she paused to look at her list—"Ellie Faneuil."

I didn't know how to feel about Rafe's new assignment.

The meeting broke up a few minutes later. As I gathered my bag to leave, Rafe came over to my side.

"I guess we'll be working together on food and drink donations for the party," he muttered, a bit sheepishly.

"Amanda made that pretty clear." I smiled as we left the meeting room and entered the darkened hallway. "She sure let you have it tonight. Although, for whatever it's worth, I agree with you."

Instead of responding, he held open the doors leading to the parking lot and asked, "What's your game plan for getting donations?"

"I thought we'd start out by calling the restaurants and markets tomorrow night. That way, we could narrow down the ones that might actually commit to a donation."

"What if we went door-to-door instead? We might have more luck if we pleaded our case in person?"

"That could take hours, Rafe, if not a couple of evenings."

"I'd rather spend the time than come up empty-handed." He smirked and mock swaggered. "Plus, I can be pretty persuasive when I try."

I smirked back. I couldn't resist saying, "Like tonight with Amanda?"

If it wasn't so dark, I felt certain that I would've seen the rugged Rafe blush. He ignored my comment and continued talking about our approach. Tomorrow during the day we'd be too busy with school to make a decision, he maintained, and we needed to hit the ground running tomorrow night.

As we strolled through the chilly parking lot toward my car, I had to laugh at the persistence—and earnestness—of Rafe's arguments. I was on the verge of agreeing to meet him in downtown Tillinghast the next night, when we came across a guy I didn't know but who seemed familiar from the larger committee meeting, sitting on the ground next to his beat-up, brown Honda. He was trying to fix a flat tire.

The night was cold and dark, and most kids would have walked right past the guy, especially if they didn't know him. At best, they might have stopped and asked if he needed help, praying that the guy declined the offer, of course. Not Rafe.

Without a single word, without a single question to the guy, Rafe handed me his backpack, took off his jacket, and rolled up his sleeves. He knelt next to the kid and asked, "What can I do?"

I watched as the two guys wordlessly replaced the punctured tire with a spare. Rafe looked even broader and stronger with his shirtsleeves rolled up; and as he worked, I couldn't help but notice how muscular his forearms were and how expertly he held a wrench. When they finished the job, I stared as they shook hands and said good-bye as if they'd known each other for years.

Rafe's instantaneous act of generosity moved me. Was it because I'd been thrown back into the completely opposite, self-centered world of Tillinghast High School? Was it because great acts of goodness and sacrifice were soon to be expected of me? Whatever the reason, I found Rafe's natural bigheartedness stirring.

Not to mention he looked amazing with his sleeves rolled up, working with his hands.

As we resumed our walk toward my car, Rafe reached out for his backpack and jacket, which I was still holding for him. He glanced at me, and asked, "You okay, Ellie? You look kind of, well, funny."

I was embarrassed at the plainness of my reaction. It was a simple tire change. The scene shouldn't have moved me so much. Nor should it have elicited an attraction to him. I had a boyfriend, after all. One that I hadn't mentioned yet, it occurred to me. For the first time, I realized how peculiar—and telling—that omission was.

I tossed my hair back over my shoulders and laughed as if his comment was preposterous. "Why wouldn't I be okay?"

Rafe slid on his jacket and backpack, and then smiled that mischievous smile. "Great. So we'll meet in Tillinghast tomorrow night?"

THIRTEEN

Rafe won the battle over our approach. Pretty easily. The next evening, we met in downtown Tillinghast at the first establishment on our list. I wanted to mention how touched I'd been by his actions the previous night helping out with the stranger's flat tire, but Rafe was all business. He didn't leave any room to discuss anything except our game plan.

We stood underneath the striped green awning of the town grocery, Smitty's. It was the oldest market in Tillinghast, one with a reputation for charity in the community. We figured we had a pretty good shot at getting a donation from Smitty's.

"What is that we'd like to get them to give us?" Rafe asked.

I checked my list. "A couple cases of soda, or a case of chips. Or both."

"I say we go for both. Are you game?"

"Definitely. Any tips on what to say?"

Rafe stepped in front of me and pulled open the door. "Let me do the talking. I think I'll do better than you."

Before I had the chance to get insulted, Rafe entered the store and asked the clerk to see the store manager. A tiny, wizened old man stepped out from the back room. A ratty, oatmeal-colored cardigan hung off his spare frame, and he pulled it tight around him in the cool air of the store.

"I'm Smitty, the store owner. Can I help you?" I was surprised that there was a real Smitty. The poor man looked ready for bed and surprised that anyone would ask to see him personally. I felt bad asking him for anything.

Rafe didn't skip a beat. He squared his very broad shoulders and stretched out his hand in greeting. "Sir, we are students from two local high schools bordering Tillinghast. I'm sure you've heard on the recent news reports about the earthquakes devastating our world—"

For the next five minutes, Rafe spun a captivating tale about the havoc the earthquakes had wreaked. Somehow, he managed to make the details horrific and compelling all at once. Even Smitty perked up and seemed mesmerized by Rafe's earnest account.

After getting a commitment for several cases of soda and two cases of chips from Smitty, we went door-to-door through Tillinghast's little downtown, trying to woo restaurants and other grocery stores for donations. Rafe was incredibly persuasive. The moment we opened the front door of whatever place was next on our list, he'd mutter something scathing to me about the party or Amanda, and then he'd flash a disarming smile to the manager we'd asked to see.

By the time we hit the last market on our list, we'd scored more food and drink donations than we could possibly use, even if everyone on our dream guest list showed up. And I'd had more fun than I'd had in a long time.

"Should we even bother?" I laughed, as we walked toward our next destination. "I'm pretty sure that we've got enough Diet Coke for every high school kid in the county. And chips too."

Rafe smiled and elbowed me in jest. "I guess we shouldn't get greedy, huh?"

"You're the one who keeps saying that a celebration isn't fitting." I elbowed him back.

"You're right." He stopped and looked at me. "We should be helping out the earthquake victims in another way."

I asked the question that had been on my mind for the past three days. "Then why did you volunteer for the party-planning subcommittee? I've spent hours listening to you and Amanda fight over the propriety of spending so much time on party decorations and music instead of a campaign to educate the partygoers. There were loads of other subcommittees to raise money *without* parties. Like Amanda said."

He smiled. "Why do you think I raised my hand? Why do you think I stayed on this subcommittee when Amanda gave me a personal invitation to leave?"

Did he mean his comment the way it sounded? My pale cheeks turned red, and I prayed that the darkness masked it. I hated to blush, especially in front of a guy. I didn't know what to say, so I kept quiet. I kept walking.

Rafe spoke instead. "Should we get a coffee instead of begging for more chips and sodas?"

I wanted to go with him. I truly did. Rafe had taken the edge off my waiting these past few days and appeased the demons of insecurity that tormented me when I was alone. I knew I shouldn't let him fill the void created by Michael's and Ruth's absences. I knew that I should sit out my solitude and anticipation until Ruth had some answers and Michael returned from the land of football. I'd had plenty of practice at being alone before I met Michael, after all.

I reminded myself of Michael, my boyfriend, my soul mate. I recounted to myself all that Michael and I were, and all that we were meant to do. I couldn't do anything to betray him, even if we weren't all that connected these days. Coffee with Rafe didn't seem right, even though it would be totally platonic. It seemed . . . deceitful.

"I'm sorry, Rafe. I—I need to get home."

His expression shifted slightly, almost indescribably. "You're right, Ellie. You have a lot on your plate. Let me walk you to your car."

Before I could answer, or ask what he meant by "a lot on my plate," he took me by the arm and walked in the exact direction of my car. How did Rafe know precisely where to go? He hadn't seen me park; we'd met at the first market on our list.

Even though part of me liked the feel of Rafe's hand on my arm, I started to get uneasy. Was he truly a regular guy? He seemed pretty normal from that flash, and I'd met a few kids from his high school on the subcommittee who knew him and appeared to like him, Amanda notwithstanding. Still, something about him unsettled me.

Even though I knew I shouldn't permit myself a flash, I wrapped my fingers around his hand, as if I'd stumbled a bit on the sidewalk. I was searching for anything out of the ordinary, any little image that suggested he was more than human. All I heard was an internal dialogue where he was beating himself up for asking me out for coffee.

Rafe was walking fast, and the street was getting darker. Out of necessity, I'd parked in an area removed from the streetlamps and foot traffic. I started to pull back, toward the slightly busier area.

As if he understood my thoughts, Rafe slowed down and said, "Sorry, Ellie. I've probably freaked you out by heading right to your spot. I saw you pull into it earlier tonight."

Of course there was a perfectly logical explanation. These days, I was pretty squirrelly. "I'm the one that's sorry, Rafe. You're just trying to be nice."

We continued walking, much slower this time, and in silence. Without the noise from the cars, it was awfully quiet. The final yards to my car felt long.

Rafe delivered me to my car door and patiently waited while I opened it. I was about to thank him and close the door, when he said, "I didn't mean to come on too strong with you, Ellie. Asking you out for coffee and all that. Sometimes, I forget how to act."

Forget how to act? What did he mean by that? But I didn't want him to feel bad—and I knew how bad he felt from the flash—so I said, "You did nothing wrong, Rafe. You asked me to grab a cup of coffee with you. That's all."

"I'm glad you feel that way, Ellie. I was hoping we could be better friends. I wanted you to understand."

Of course, that was all. Aside from asking me out for coffee, which *any* friend could do, Rafe had never done anything to encourage me. I had no concrete reason to think he liked me, other than the flash I'd gotten from him in the gymnasium and the one I'd sought just now. And both of those could have been interpreted other ways. I should've been relieved, but I wasn't.

"That's great, Rafe." Even though part of me thought it was definitely not great.

"Good. Then I'll see you tomorrow in the early evening in town for some follow-up work on these donations?"

"Tomorrow evening."

Fourteen

That night, I couldn't sleep again. Thoughts of Rafe and Michael and the prophecy spun a web in my mind. Not the eerie futuristic dreams to which I'd grown accustomed or the disquieting nightmares about the man with the black hair. Instead, I had a vivid dream in which Rafe, Michael, and I flew the skies together in a mad race to halt the ticking of the end-days clock. By the time morning arrived, I was so confused.

I mean, how could I simultaneously dream about Rafe, love Michael, and worry about the end of the world?

That morning, I drove myself to school instead of riding in with Michael. I needed a car for my meeting in town with Rafe just before Michael's Friday night football game. In lieu of our car ride, Michael and I planned on meeting at my locker before class. Normally, I was excited to have my few minutes alone with Michael in the morning, but today I felt something very different as I approached locker number twenty-four. Dread.

As if I'd betrayed Michael by enjoying my time with Rafe. Like he once betrayed me.

We couldn't afford this distraction. So I pretended nothing was out of the ordinary, something I'd gotten awfully good at doing. I painted on my smile as I walked down the hallway toward my locker, where Michael was waiting, and kept my lighthearted banter going for a while once we met. Only when he leaned in to kiss me good-bye did I start to tense up. Would he be able to read my conflicting thoughts about Rafe through our kiss?

At the same moment his lips lightly touched mine, I felt a tap on my shoulder. I spun around to see Ruth. I was never so thankful to have an intimate moment interrupted.

"Sorry, guys, but I needed to catch you both," she said, blushing at having to disturb us.

"Don't worry, Ruth," I rushed to reassure her. "What's up?"

"I think I found something. Can you meet after school today?"

"Of course," I said, immediately relieved at the thought that the waiting might be over. I'd have to cancel my meeting with Rafe, but I felt a certain relief about that too. Maybe if he was out of sight, he'd be out of mind. I really, really needed him to be out of mind.

"I can't," Michael said.

Ruth and I stared at each other—and then at Michael—in surprise. What could possibly take precedence over this?

"What?" I asked.

"It's Friday. I have a game. Remember?" He actually sounded irritated that we'd forgotten about his football game.

"Right. Football," I said.

"You are coming to the game, aren't you?"

"Of course. But couldn't you meet us beforehand?" I was incredulous. How could he think about football at a time like this? Maybe it was the little sideline fan club that he couldn't do without.

"Ellie, you know that Coach Samuel has the team eat an early dinner together then has a strategy meeting before the game. Can't we meet after the game?" He was intractable. "The team is counting on me, Ellie."

"It's not exactly like we've got limitless time, Michael. And a *lot* more people than those on your football team are counting on us. Remember?" My tone was every bit as irritated as his.

I could tell that he was about to retort—sharply and uncharacteristically—when Ruth interjected, "Why don't we meet at the Daily Grind *after* the football game? I don't think a few extra hours will make that much difference."

"Are you sure, Ruth?" I asked.

"I think so."

"Can you make it there after the game, Michael?" Even though I tried to ask him pleasantly, the annoyance hadn't altogether disappeared from my voice. It was clear Michael heard it too.

"Yes, Ellie. I'll be there," Michael said before storming off.

Ruth and I rolled our eyes in disbelief at Michael's behavior. Even though I knew that Michael and I were supposed to act normally, his slavish insistence on playing football and his concern for the team was beyond normal. He'd never been so gung ho about it before.

What was happening to *my* Michael? One of the things that drew me to him initially was his inner confidence. He did what he wanted—what seemed meaningful and true to him—without worrying about the social consequences. Like spend Saturday night at the Odeon movie theater watching an indie film all by himself. Something no self-respecting upperclassman would do, especially not a football player. Now he seemed strangely motivated by the impact of his actions on our classmates and his team. Almost to the exclusion of our *real* goal. He wasn't simply playacting a normal teen anymore.

I debated discussing this change with Ruth. Certainly,

she had to have noticed the alterations in his personality over recent days. On balance, I decided against it. Ruth had enough on her plate without worrying about problems between me and Michael. The ones who were supposed to be saving the world.

FIFTEEN

I cancelled my meeting with Rafe and confirmed plans with Ruth to go to Michael's game after our fight. It seemed the right thing to do, even though I definitely didn't feel like witnessing the adoration from the fans or Michael's own blind devotion to the game. For the first time since we started dating, I hadn't seen him in the hallways between classes, and I knew he must be avoiding me. We needed to be in sync in the coming days, so I needed to forgive him. After all, I had done some things deserving forgiveness too, although he didn't know about them. Like dreaming about Rafe.

After killing some time in the library after school, Ruth and I headed over to nearby Bethel High School stadium in our separate cars. The stands were packed, as Tillinghast was playing its fierce rival team from the rural Bethel Township. We had to jockey for seats in the bleachers among the hundreds of students, parents, teachers, and local supporters.

Even though I'd seen Michael run out onto the field before, for some reason, the way he looked struck me. His physicality reminded me of all our long nights together. Long nights that seemed a long time away. He literally took my breath away. I held it, waiting to see what he would do.

The first few plays disappointed, but not because of Michael. Again and again, Michael was in position as wide receiver. Still, none of the other players managed to pass him the ball. I watched as the clock ticked down to the end of the first quarter, and I could feel the frustration in the fans around me.

Then, with seconds left in the first quarter, the center tossed the ball to the quarterback. The quarterback held the ball tightly in his grip and readied his throw. He scanned the field, looking for one of his guys to be open. Most of his players were caught up with Bethel's team near the end zone. All except Michael.

I saw the quarterback nod in Michael's direction, and then release the ball. As Michael prepared himself to catch the pass, a massive pileup of guys landed right in front of him. The football sailed through the air toward Michael, but it seemed impossible that Michael could jump high enough to catch it.

Until he did.

I watched as Michael lifted off from the ground with

grace and speed. I'd only ever seen him get such height during our late-night meetings.

The crowd cheered wildly as Michael caught the ball in midair and scored a touchdown. As he ran back to the sidelines, I watched the back of his coach's head as he reached out to give Michael a high five. Michael's face shone with pleasure at the roar of the fans. I saw that Michael wasn't thinking at all about the end days or Nephilim or even me. He was reveling in his own glory. Reflected glory, that was, from the coach, his teammates, and the fans.

But there was more, and I was furious.

"Wow, Ellie, Michael is amazing tonight." Ruth interrupted my thoughts. I heard awe in her voice.

"Yeah, he's amazing, all right."

The anger in my voice was irrepressible, and Ruth turned to me in surprise. I didn't dare explain why I was so mad at him. I knew what everyone else didn't.

Michael had used his powers on the field.

SIXTEEN

How *dare* Michael? After all his lecturing about our not using our powers—not even to figure out this end-days puzzle—to protect ourselves and our parents from the other fallen angels, Michael had used his powers for a high school football game. It was unbelievable.

The more I thought about it, the madder I got. Anger always made me quiet, which Ruth understood all too well. When I was silent on the walk from the stadium to the parking lot, she knew better than to ask why. Even though I'm sure she was insatiably curious for the details.

We hopped into our separate cars, fortunately for Ruth. The ride alone to the Daily Grind gave me time to think. I was still furious at the risk Michael had taken, yet I knew we needed to be aligned. Maybe he had a good reason for clinging to his football successes, I told myself, and I simply didn't understand it. Even though, for the life of me, I couldn't conjure up an acceptable explanation for his using his powers on the field. By the time Ruth and I met up at the coffee shop, I had cooled off enough to be civil and wait patiently for Michael.

Ruth and I watched as the coffee house clock hit nine, nine thirty, and then ten, all the while making pathetic attempts at small talk. Michael never showed. I called him repeatedly on his cell. He never picked up. All my hard-won equanimity started to slip away. It was one thing for Michael to punish me with the cold shoulder, but it was an entirely different thing for him to ignore his enormous responsibility to humankind because he was mad at me. After all we'd been through in Boston, how could he disregard the stakes?

"I don't think we should wait any longer, Ellie," Ruth finally whispered.

"I know, Ruth." I sighed. "Talk to me. What did you find?"

She passed me one of her famous binders. Flipping it open, I faced charts and graphs and statistics, as well as a few heavily highlighted newspaper articles. My head was still too muddled with anger at Michael to sort through it all.

"Can you give me the layman's version?" I asked.

Ruth laughed; it was the first sign of levity from either one of us since we arrived at the Daily Grind. She whispered, "Sure. As you know, there are six seals left. If you disregard the final seal—the emergence of a very scary end-days leader—we have famine, widespread disease, economic depression, revolutions, and persecution of Christians."

She sounded like she was spouting off a grocery list. A very terrifying grocery list.

"Wonderful," I said.

Ruth ignored my cynicism and plowed ahead. "I looked at worldwide trends and anticipated environmental events. And at first, nothing jumped out at me as a potential sign. Then I came across a few articles predicting a potentially catastrophic climatic event." She pointed to the articles in the binder that were covered with yellow highlighter.

"What was that?"

"There's this enormous volcano under a glacier on an island off the coast of Greenland. Most people ignore it, because you can't see it and it has only erupted two times in the past couple of thousand years."

"Yes . . ." I said, waiting for the other shoe to drop.

"Well, in the past few months, it began rumbling."

"Rumbling?"

"Yes, rumbling. Even though the volcano's workings are too mysterious to make definite predictions, the articles put together some scientific data suggesting that it will erupt. Very soon."

I thought back to Ruth's tutorial on the Book of Revelation, and I felt relieved. Disease, famine, revolutions, economic crisis, and persecution of believers made the end-days list. Yet, I didn't recall her mentioning volcanoes. "A volcanic eruption isn't one of the seven seals."

Ruth shook her head, and the look in her eyes was of a quiet intensity. "No, it isn't. But, if that volcano erupts, do you know what will happen?"

I was almost afraid to ask. "What?"

"The articles describe an enormous ash cloud that will drift over Europe and Northern Africa. At first, airline flights will be canceled across the two continents, since it's unsafe to fly with all that debris in the air. It will seem a nuisance for travelers and a financial threat to the travel business. Then, a domino effect will occur. Necessary medical supplies will be unable to reach hospitals and doctors, resulting in the spread of disease. The food business, which depends on air cargo shipments to deliver its products to consumers and markets, will suffer; and vast quantities of produce and refrigerated products will spoil. If the ash cloud is thick enough, the sun will be blocked, leading to loss of crops and farm animals. This would inevitably yield a food crisis."

"Oh my God, the volcano will break open at least two of the seals at once: famine and disease."

"Potentially."

"How likely is this volcano to erupt? And when?"

Ruth opened the binder and drew my attention to one of her many charts. "Very likely. Scientists think it will happen quite soon."

"Why haven't we seen any of this in the news?"

"No one is looking for it. Except us."

I took a look down at the articles. I'd been too engrossed in Ruth's delivery to give them more than a cursory glance. "Hold on a second, Ruth. These articles are all from newspapers like *Year 2012: End of the World.*"

She nodded. "I know. It looks like the ravings of some conspiratorial, doomsday kook, right?"

I nodded back.

"To be sure it made sense, I showed this stuff to my dad. He said that sometimes these publications are right on the money. They'll take reporting risks that the big news houses won't. Plus, he checked out the science, and he said it looked pretty sound."

"You talked about this to your dad?" I couldn't keep the anger from my voice. How could Ruth not understand the critical importance of secrecy?

"Calm down, Ellie. I told him that I had a school project to try to identify the next major environmental catastrophe. You know, on the heels of the earthquakes. He was all over it."

"All right," I said hesitantly. "Thanks for all your hard work on this, Ruth."

Ruth gave me a small smile; even though the news was troubling, she was clearly proud of her efforts. While I appreciated them, her delight surprised me. I wondered if she had forgotten what would happen to *all* of us if she was right.

"Did your dad also tell you how we can stop a volcano?"

The smile disappeared. "Well, we can't stop the volcano itself."

"That's what I figured."

"But," she hastened to add, "we can prevent some of the more significant devastation. We might be able to stave off the famine or some of the more virulent diseases. That way, we would be able to stop at least a couple of the seals from breaking."

"And how would we go about that?"

Ruth pointed to her binder again. "By showing this to the authorities. So they can prepare against food shortages or a health crisis."

"So, Michael and I would waltz into the White House with your binder, and they'd immediately mobilize the foreign governments." I shook my head incredulously. "No government on the planet is going to listen to the apocalyptic warnings of two teenagers."

Ruth looked down at her lap. I'd taken all the wind out of her sails with my criticism, and I felt bad. As I started to apologize, she said quietly, "True. Maybe no one would listen to two regular teenagers. What about two teenagers who can fly?"

Ruth had a point. I bet some authority figures would take a few minutes to peruse Ruth's binder if Michael and I flew into their offices, before they hustled us off to a scientific lab for examination. If Michael and I revealed our true natures, we would not only risk our freedom but also the main thing we were trying to protect by pretending to be normal—our parents. Then again, maybe Michael had already taken that risk by using his powers on the football field. I was confused and overwhelmed, and I desperately needed to talk to Michael.

Where was he?

"Michael promised me I wouldn't be alone in all this," I whispered, mostly to myself.

Ruth reached over and gave me a big hug. The sympathy forced my guard down even further. And I'd been working so hard to keep it up.

"What's going on with you guys, Ellie? You and Michael seem so mad at each other."

My voice quivered a little. So much for being a strong, biblical creature. "I still love him, Ruth. The real Michael, the one I met a couple of months ago. But right now, I don't understand him. And I really don't like him. He's changed so much recently. Haven't you noticed?" It felt disloyal to say aloud the words that had been running through my mind.

Ruth was reluctant to answer; I could tell. Still, I needed to know what she thought. Had I become fickle? Were Michael and I just growing apart naturally, not because of any big alteration in his personality? Was something—or someone—coming between us?

"Please, Ruth. Tell me what you think," I asked again.

"Of course, I've noticed, Ellie. He's way into football, much more than he ever was before. That seems strange under the circumstances. And he's so good at acting normal that it sometimes seems like he's forgotten that all this supernatural stuff happened. It's almost like he's—" She stopped, clearly fearful of going too far. Michael was still my boyfriend, after all.

"Yes?" I prompted her.

"It's almost like he's lost his compassion," Ruth said slowly.

"I know," I answered quietly, letting the sad truth of the words sink in. "I mean, the other night Rafe and I were walking through the school parking lot, and without even blinking, he went over to help some stranger fix his flat tire. The old Michael would have done exactly the same thing—help out another human being in need. I'm not so certain about this new Michael. Would he be too worried about being late for practice?"

Ruth looked at me with eyes askance. "Who's Rafe?"

"Just some guy I met at that committee to raise money for the earthquake victims."

"You don't say his name like he's 'just some guy.'"

"Well, he is . . ." I said, sounding defensive even to my own ears. "We've been working together on getting food donations for the big fund-raiser."

Ruth's voice grew low and deadly serious. She looked scared. "Ellie, you cannot let anyone come between you and Michael, no matter how confused you are about him right now. No matter how crazy obsessed he is with football. You cannot mess up things with the guy who's supposed to help you save the world."

"I won't, Ruth. I promise. When I look into Michael's eyes, I know that he is my soul mate. And I know we will stand together when the end comes," I said to placate Ruth. And myself.

SEVENTEEN

Ruth and I left the familiar warmth of the Daily Grind and stepped outside. It was dark, and the near emptiness of downtown Tillinghast surprised me at first. Then I realized it was almost eleven. Most high school kids headed home after the football game, and most college students probably stuck to parties on campus. It seemed like only Ruth and I braved the Tillinghast streets.

We had parked in opposite directions. The autumn cold was bracing, so Ruth and I gave each other a quick hug before racing off to our cars. Even though we promised to talk through our strategy in the morning, I felt entirely alone. How would I make it through the long night hours ahead of me, thinking about Ruth's news, without knowing Michael's whereabouts?

He hadn't returned my calls. Was he still mad about that morning? We had been through so much together—had been intimate in ways others could never imagine—and

I found it unfathomable that he would harbor so silly a grudge. Especially now. After all, I wasn't mad anymore, even though I had a lot to be angry about. Like his having used his powers on the football field.

Serious concerns over his welfare started to creep into my mind. Was Michael okay? Had someone hurt him, on the field or off? Like one of the fallen?

I'd been so angry with him that I hadn't considered the possibility that he *couldn't* pick up my calls. I thought about my parting words to Ruth about Michael and me standing together, and I suddenly felt incredibly guilty. If I was truly standing by him, I would be making sure that he was safe, above all else.

Grabbing my bag off my shoulder, I rummaged for my phone. My hand shook with nerves as I hit the speed dial for Michael. While I listened to his cell ring, praying that he'd pick up, the distant thud of footsteps penetrated my consciousness. They sounded far away at first. Yet very quickly, they grew closer.

I spun around, ready to confront my pursuer. Or fly away. I was part angel, after all.

But the street was empty.

It was probably someone running to his car in the cold. I was acting as paranoid as I had last night with Rafe. Not that I didn't have just cause these days. As I turned down the side street where I'd parked my car, I kept thinking that Ruth and I should've walked together to one of our cars and then driven to the other.

My thoughts returned to Michael, and I tried him another time. Once again, he didn't pick up. It was too late to call his house, but I had to risk angering his parents. I had to find out if he was all right. At the same moment that I dialed the final digit of his home number, I heard a voice behind me.

"Spare any change, miss?"

I turned around to see a grubby-looking man on the stoop of a closed stationery store. He was holding out a can and a small, hand-lettered sign, and he was shivering visibly in the cold night air. I hadn't noticed him before. Then again, he certainly wasn't seated at eye level.

I started to recoil from his appearance, from my own fears about strangers, from the unknown end-day dangers that threatened us. Then the word "hypocrite" passed through my mind. How could I beg for donations to help out some faraway earthquake victims, when I wouldn't even give some money to a poor, downtrodden guy right in my own town? How could I accuse Michael of lacking compassion, when I wouldn't show any myself?

Quickly, I stuck my hand back into my purse. As I rooted around for my wallet, he said, "Thanks, miss. Anything you can give will help."

"Good luck to you," I said, as I deposited a handful of change and a few stray dollar bills into his can. Then I backed away and headed toward my car. Fast. Even without the end days looming and supernatural creatures abounding, the scene was a little creepy.

"Would you like to help even more, Ellspeth?" he called out behind me.

I spun around. He was no man. Even from this distance, I could see his eyes had changed. There was an intensity there that was otherworldly. He was a fallen angel.

How could I be so stupid? So gullible?

I started running. As I rounded the bend to my car, I bumped right into him. The fallen loomed before me. He was much faster than me, so fast I hadn't even seen him move ahead of me.

He no longer looked grubby, even though he still wore his costume of a homeless person. In fact, he was breathtaking. Dark golden curls framed his flawless face, and his fair skin looked like porcelain. He was beautiful, uncannily evocative of a Michelangelo angel. Perhaps he had served as the inspiration centuries ago. I'd certainly never seen his like walking an earthly street.

His finger reached out to stroke my cheek. Even though his touch was gentle, I writhed away in trepidation. Fallen angels were notorious for their ability to sway others through touch and voice, and I'd been lured in before by the wiles of the fallen. Regardless, when he next spoke, his tone so intoxicated me that I had to submit to his caress. And his words.

"Please listen to me, Ellspeth. My name is Kael. I know you're scared, but you have nothing to fear from me. The fallen are not the malicious creatures that you think. In fact, with you at our side, we could do so much to help humankind. We could spare humankind so much suffering—disease, hunger, the very kinds of anguish you are trying to alleviate in the earthquake victims. We've been waiting for you."

I started to pull away, until I heard him speak again. His persuasive powers were out in full force.

"For long, long centuries—for millennia, even—we tried to hasten the prophecy that a Nephilim would return. Despite His explicit prohibition, we attempted to create you, our beloved child. Endlessly it seemed, we searched for you among the newborn humans, hoping that one of our kind had been successful. Time and time again, we found nothing. We began to lose hope.

"Then we began to sense you. Feel the emergence of your wondrous powers—flight, insights, the call of the blood. Yet your so-called parents masked you well. So well that our hunt proved fruitless for many years. It took the surfacing of your dear friend Michael, with his tie to my lost brother Ezekiel, to lead us to you."

Kael paused. It seemed that he had reached his ultimate supplication. I was under his power, and all I could do was listen.

"Ellspeth, we have been waiting for you so that we—fallen and Nephilim alike—can win back our place on earth and in heaven. And take our place as benevolent rulers of humanity." The fallen touched my cheek once again. "Come, my child. You belong with us. Don't leave humankind to the despair of its own devices, to the suffering that surely awaits without us."

His words, his touch, and his beauty enthralled. Even the compassion of his message. Instead of fighting back, as I knew I should, I found myself listening and succumbing. It sounded enticing to stand at the side of powerful beings and free humankind from pain and suffering. Even though a distant part of me knew that this play on my empathy must be part of his game.

The fallen stretched out his free hand for mine. I lifted my hand. As my fingers grazed his, I felt a whoosh over my head. It broke the spell, and instinctively, I ducked. Kael was left standing alone. Until he was plucked from the sky.

I didn't pause to see who had taken Kael or what had become of him. I dashed down the street toward my car.

For a split second, I couldn't decide whether to drive or fly away. The car might be too slow, but I didn't want to risk running into any of the fallen in the skies. As I fumbled in my bag for the keys, I heard a terrible fight break out over my head.

I looked upward. Although I could hear an unnatural shrieking and the crash of bodies, I couldn't tell who was fighting with Kael in the darkness. So I turned my attention back to more important things, like finding my keys, opening my car door, and getting away.

Finally, finally, I felt my keys, grabbed them, and turned the car lock. The moment I did, the skies grew silent. As I slid into the car, I glanced upward once last time. No one was there. Where had Kael and the other being gone? I couldn't hesitate long enough to find out. This was my chance to escape.

I started to close my car door, but then I felt a hand on my arm. Despite my efforts to wrench it free, the hand held me fast and pulled me out of the dark car into the dimly lit streets.

A familiar voice said, "Ellie, don't be scared. It's me."

I thought Michael had finally surfaced. Just in time.

I was wrong.

It was Rafe.

EIGHTEEN

"What on earth are you doing here?"

Those were the first words that popped out of my mouth. The second I blurted them out, I wanted to reel them back in. I didn't want to sound accusatory when, in fact, I was incredibly grateful to see a friendly human face, after the scare I'd had.

I took a good, hard look at Rafe. Inexplicably, he was calm and smiling. What had happened? When had he stumbled onto this scene? I assumed that he'd seen something of the aerial fight, so why wasn't he freaked out by what he'd observed?

His tone tranquil and his face composed, he answered me. "I could tell you that it was coincidence. That I happened to be strolling down the streets of Tillinghast in the hopes of bumping into you after the game and found you under attack."

Even though his expression didn't look ominous,

there was something unnerving in his even-keeled tone. Something I recognized enough to make me scared. He hadn't stumbled onto the scene. What role had he played in it?

"That wouldn't be true, would it?" I asked, even though I already knew the answer.

"No, Ellspeth. That wouldn't be true. It would be a lie. And I think you know how I feel about lies."

Ellspeth. Why was Rafe calling me Ellspeth? He only knew me as Ellie. I rarely shared my full name with anyone.

The pieces were starting to come together, and my fears were mounting. Had I escaped one threat only to land smack-dab in the middle of another? I started to back away from him. Slowly.

"Are you one of them?" Silently, I prayed that Rafe was not another fallen, that he was a regular, run-of-the-mill stalker. A stalker, I could handle.

"One of who?" he answered.

Rafe moved toward me, just as slowly.

"One of the fallen," I said, as I continued my backward progress.

"I'm not fallen, Ellspeth."

Unexpectedly, Rafe stopped walking toward me. Ever so slightly, he shook himself. The action was so unusual and startling that I stopped my retreat to watch. What on earth was he doing?

A cloud of luminous particles were emitted from him. When it cleared, I saw a very different Rafe. It was as if he'd shaken all the scruffiness and roughness—all the humanity, really—off him. His hair was still chestnut brown, his features remained the same, and his eyes were still near black, but I almost didn't recognize him. His face had become even more beautiful than before, nearly exquisite. He looked ageless, even divine.

Then he gave me his disarming smile, and I saw the Rafe I knew.

"Who are you? What are you?" I asked, after I shut my gaping mouth.

"I'm an angel. My full name is Raphael."

"You're a regular angel? From heaven?" I felt ridiculous even saying the words aloud.

"Yes. An angel of His presence, to be more specific," he answered, as if my question amused him. "That makes me one of the few angels permitted to stand before Him."

My head was spinning way too fast to pose more questions about the lofty-sounding "angel of His presence." But I definitely needed to know one thing for certain. "What happened to Kael?"

"He's gone, Ellie."

"Gone for the moment, or gone forever?"

"Gone forever."

"You killed him?" I asked slowly. While I was disgusted with myself for almost believing Kael's line about joining forces so we could help save humankind, and loathed Kael for it, it felt wrong that he should be killed on my behalf.

"No, Ellie. But he won't come back for you again. I made sure of that."

Before I could ask Rafe exactly how he "made sure of that," a very, very troubling thought occurred to me. "How can I be certain that you are not one of the fallen?"

Rafe, or Raphael—I didn't know what to call him, even in my own mind—stuck out his arm. "There's only one way to be certain."

"Your blood?"

"Yes." He said very matter-of-factly.

"Angels have blood?"

He smiled. "We are all made in His image."

"You want me to drink your blood?" I was dumbfounded.

"Only through my blood can you be certain of who I am."

"I don't know, Rafe. I stole some flashes off you, and you seemed pretty normal in them. Maybe you can fake your blood too."

"It's not possible, Ellspeth. Surely you know that."

I looked down at his muscled forearm, knowing he was right. Blood was too pure to fake, you couldn't make blood lie.

I shivered at the very thought of tasting his blood. What if he was fallen? Would he have some control over me if I ingested his blood? There were too many unknowns, plus I'd never bitten anyone other than Michael. The whole prospect felt like cheating on Michael.

I knew that I had to do it. How else could I be certain that Rafe was an angel and not a fallen?

Taking his arm in my hands, I closed my eyes and brought my lips to his skin. I bared my teeth and tried to bite down, but couldn't. It felt all wrong.

"Go ahead, Ellspeth. It's okay," Rafe said gently.

Forcing myself to push past my fears, my teeth pierced his skin. The warm liquid rushed into my mouth. It tasted unlike anything I'd ever experienced. It transmitted a sensation unlike anything I'd ever felt. As his blood coursed through me, warmth and light pulsed through my body and mind and spirit. And peace. It felt like I'd tumbled down onto the softest feather bed in the world, and then fallen into the deepest, loveliest sleep. Sleep that I never, ever wanted to awaken from. I knew—without question— that I was experiencing divine peace.

"Do you believe me?"

"Yes, I do," I answered groggily, as if waking from a dream. The sense of the divine lingered.

"Good."

"Although, your blood didn't tell me why you're here."

"He gave me this job."

"Who's he?"

"The Maker, God, Yahweh, the Creator—whatever name you'd like to give to Him." Rafe's smile turned wry. For all his otherworldliness, he still bore that intangible, slightly mischievous quality that I first saw in the Tillinghast gymnasium, the quality I really liked.

When I didn't respond, he continued. "Although, until you meet Him in person, it's hard to come up with the right name for Him. I see why humans have struggled with that. Anyway, He's very different than He's been described."

"What do you do for Him?"

"I look after the earth and the spirits of all humankind."

"By participating in high school fund-raisers?" I blurted out, and then covered my mouth. I had forgotten I was speaking to an angel.

Rafe did not take offense at my question. In fact, he seemed downright entertained by it.

Then he reassembled his face into a serious expression and answered my question quite gravely. He clearly had a message to impart. "By making sure that you understand the importance of your role as the Elect One."

"That's why you came here? For me?"

"Yes, Ellspeth. I've been watching you since the day you were born, waiting to see if you would rise to your role. That's probably why it's so hard for me to call you by anything other than your birth name of Ellspeth. I've always thought of you by your full name. When the end days began, I decided to come to earth. To help you. Even though I haven't walked on ground myself since the time of Noah."

My jaw dropped at his words. Again. "Since the time of Noah?"

The amused smile disappeared from Rafe's face, as he said, "Yes, Ellspeth. I was here when the first angels fell and when the first Nephilim were created. I was here in the beginning."

NINETEEN

Rafe started his story as if he had always meant to share it with me. Although with Rafe, the word "always" took on entirely new meaning.

"In the beginning of time, God sent two hundred angels to earth with a specific mission. He wanted them to guide humankind and to protect them from the threats on earth and from their own souls," Rafe said. The humor was completely gone from his face.

His story sounded familiar. I had read bits and pieces of this tale before in Genesis and the Book of Enoch and the Book of Jubilees. Yet reading the words on a page was incredibly different than hearing them spoken aloud by an angel who had been there himself.

"When the two hundred got here, led by the chief angel Samyaza, they found the human men and women to be incredibly beautiful. And why not? They were made in His image. They were luminous. And innocent.

"That innocence made them irresistible to the angels. It brewed in the angels a desire to teach humans all their secrets. Secrets about the earth and themselves that God explicitly forbade them to share. He didn't think his new creations were ready yet.

"The angels defied Him. They taught humankind to read the stars and understand the cycles of the moon. Men and women were told how to farm and exploit the land. The angels revealed the use of currency and coin. Azaziel, one of the chief angels under Samyaza, dared to teach the most closely guarded secret of all."

"What was that?"

"War. Azaziel educated men and women in the art of war."

"War? Why would angels even know about war?"

"God has always given His creations a choice between light and dark, good and evil. Angels are no exception. When His creations go about making that choice, war breaks out. Azaziel became especially good at it. And fond of it." Rafe uttered Azaziel's name with particular distaste.

Rafe's story wasn't quite over. "These two hundred angels enjoyed revealing these secrets to humankind. They found it to be heady and exhilarating—almost godlike. And they didn't stop at that. They went even further." He paused.

"What did they do?" I asked the question to prompt him along, even though I thought I knew the answer. I needed to hear the whole story from Rafe. From someone who'd been there.

"Remember that the angels found humans to be beautiful. They had relationships with human men and women. And, they had children with them. Half man, half angel. Nephilim."

"Like me."

"Like you. And not like you." He smiled his old smile, and added, "No one is quite like you, Ellspeth."

Rafe inhaled deeply, and the humor faded. I could see that this next part of the story was difficult for him to share.

"From above, my brother and sister angels watched this behavior of the two hundred. We were shocked by the angels' flagrant disregard of God's instructions. Who did they think they were, revealing His secrets? The secrets weren't theirs to share. And how dare they procreate with humans?

"But God did nothing.

"I—along with Gabriel, Suriel, Michael, and Uriel—went to God. We pointed out the disobedience and the disrespect of the angels' acts. Then we dared to ask Him, What was He planning to do?" Rafe paused, seemingly lost in his remembrances.

He didn't quickly resume. The pause grew so long that I finally decided to prompt him further. "What did God say?"

"He asked if we thought they should be punished. When we answered yes, God asked us how. We suggested that He banish the two hundred to earth, to allow them their powers but forbid them access to heaven. God agreed, and of His own accord, went one step further. He wanted to teach the rebellious angels a lesson, and humankind along with them. He commanded the Flood to destroy all their followers and all their children."

"You and the other angels must have been relieved. He gave you what you asked for."

"Yes, at first. Quickly, however, we learned that the punishment didn't have the effect we'd hoped for. The Dark Fallen—as we came to call them—didn't feel remorse for their acts. Instead, they felt vengeful, because He had killed their children and taken away their ability to enter heaven. So as their means of revenge, they continued to disobey Him by continuing their forbidden activities."

"Do you regret the punishment you inflicted?" It felt unnatural asking an angel about his regrets. Yet that was what I thought I saw on Rafe's face.

"Yes, for its outcome and for its harshness. We were too severe. The Dark Fallen turned away from the light and power of God to celebrate themselves when they taught humankind and created the Nephilim. Their acts went against His teachings. But that's not why I think that I was too harsh in my punishment of the fallen."

"Why do you think you were too strict with them?"

Rafe took me by the hands and looked at me with his beautiful eyes. I couldn't have broken away from his gaze if I'd wanted to. And I didn't want to.

"At first, I believed that the fallen acted solely from the sin of pride. Pride in their ability to teach and to create, like God. Pride in their own power and egos. I should have shown more compassion. Because I now understand how the fallen fell. It wasn't pride alone. It was I—" He stopped himself.

Abruptly he released my hands and backed away. "It doesn't matter why the fallen fell, and how I feel about their punishment is unimportant. It's old news now. Preventing the fallen from exacting their final vengeance, however, *is* critical. That is the destiny you share with Michael."

"I don't think Michael is speaking to me right now."

"You must go to him and repair this rift between you. Only together can you stop the coming devastation."

I grabbed back one of his hands and asked, "Will you help me? Help us?"

Rafe looked at me sadly and said, "I wish I could. I've

already done far too much. I was only meant to observe. All I can do now is watch and pray."

"Please, Rafe. I don't know what to do. I don't know how to stop the end days. Michael is as ignorant as me."

"I don't know, Ellspeth," he said slowly.

"Are you fearful that God will punish you for disobeying him? Like he punished the two hundred?"

The mischief that I'd seen in his eyes before reappeared. "No, I'm pretty sure that I can talk Him out of that. This is definitely different."

"Then please, Rafe. Please help us."

He leaned toward me again and, for a fleeting moment, I wished he would kiss me. Until I reminded myself who he was and who I was.

Instead, Rafe lightly caressed my cheek—more like a brother this time—and said, "Maybe I can do one last thing. . . ."

TWENTY

I stood in the backyard outside Michael's house, staring up at his bedroom window. I didn't dare fly up to his room, even though there didn't seem to be much reason to hide my powers anymore. Pretending to be normal hadn't stopped the end days. Yet Rafe had asked that I refrain for a bit longer, and I couldn't refuse the request of an angel.

Instead, feeling like some kind of lovesick Shakespearean character, I threw a pebble at Michael's window. His face instantly appeared through the glass. At first, he merely looked startled to see me. Then I saw anger and confusion pass across his face like a storm cloud. When I motioned for him to come outside, I feared that he'd refuse. But he didn't; he left the window and headed downstairs.

Michael stepped out onto his porch. Even in the darkness, I could see the sheen of his white-blond hair and the outline of his broad shoulders. In my mind's eye, I filled in the details of his green eyes and sculpted arms and chest.

I longed for him. I wanted *my* Michael back, the soul mate with whom I spent long nights flying and talking and kissing and sharing everything. Those nights were the happiest of my life, and now they seemed a lifetime away.

I waited as Michael closed the back door quietly behind him. He hesitantly crossed the yard and approached the tree I stood under. Drawing near me, he still didn't reach out to hug or kiss me as he usually did. The distance between us made me incredibly sad. It was depressing what had happened to our relationship over the course of a few short weeks.

I was determined to put all this baffling discord behind us, and not only because Rafe asked me to. I had even vowed not to mention the infuriating use of his powers on the football field. Reaching out to embrace him, I said, "I'm sorry we fought."

Michael's body stiffened at first. Slowly, I felt his body soften and then relent. He wrapped his arms around me. "Me too."

I luxuriated in the circle of his arms for a few long minutes. The yearning for Michael and his blood started to build, and I pulled back a tiny bit. Enough to study his eyes. I needed to make sure that *my* Michael inhabited them, not that scary automaton he'd become under Ezekiel's influence or the withdrawn, confusing football player he'd become recently.

I was relieved. In his incandescent green eyes, I saw only the Michael I loved.

"I'm not sure what happened earlier today. I—" I started to say.

Michael interrupted me. "I'm the one that's been acting like a jerk. I've been so caught up in—"

It was my turn to quiet him. I traced my finger over the curve of his full lips and said, "You don't have to explain, Michael. We've both been caught up."

"Not like me, Ellie. I've been so wrapped up with football and Coach Samuel. More than ever before. Not like I was with Ezekiel—I promised you that would never happen again—but definitely distracted. I mean, I even allowed myself to stay after the game with the coach to run through plays, instead of meeting you and Ruth, even when I knew she had important news. Then I ignored your calls because I was still pissed that you made fun of me playing football." He shook his head in disbelief at his own actions. "I have no excuse, only an apology."

Looking into the anguish and remorse on his face, I knew I'd been right not to chastise him for using his powers in the game. Michael was already beating himself up for his behavior; he didn't need me to berate him also.

I hugged him tighter, and said, "There is no need to

apologize. Not anymore. We're together again."

He squeezed me so hard that I could hardly breathe. "Thank God for that. So, what did Ruth say?"

"A volcano on an island off the coast of Greenland is about to erupt, and—"

"There are no volcanoes mentioned in Revelation," he interjected.

"I know. Ruth believes that this volcano will have big consequences, among them disease and famine. And those disasters *are* referenced—"

He interrupted again, "In Revelation. Oh my God, what do we do?"

I smiled at him reassuringly. "I've brought help."

"By help I hope you don't mean Ruth. No offense to Ruth." Michael looked skeptical at the amount of help Ruth could offer beyond her research.

"No, I brought someone a bit more powerful than Ruth." Turning to the trees lining the perimeter of Michael's yard, I whispered loudly, "Rafe?"

Rafe emerged from the trees behind Michael's house. With his brawny physique and dark hair, he was still handsome, but he no longer bore that angelic quality. As we had driven from the Tillinghast town center to Michael's house, the dust of humanity had descended upon him once again. Wearing his usual flannel shirt and scruffy jeans,

Rafe looked every bit a real teenager.

They sized each other up. It was bizarre watching these two men in my life—if you could even call them men, given that they were much more than human—assess each other.

Every muscle in Michael's body tensed, as if readying for a battle. Even though I let my arms slacken a bit, I held him close. The next few minutes were critical, and I needed Michael to have faith in me. I knew this would be tough for him, the last time someone new convinced us to let him "help," it was Ezekiel. And here I was, foisting some unknown teenage guy on him.

"Who is this?" Michael said, as warily as I predicted.

"This is Rafe. I met him at a committee to help the earthquake victims."

Michael was immediately furious. He allowed me no leeway for explanation. "Why would you bring some stranger over to my house in the middle of the night? Especially at a time like this?"

"Because he's not some stranger."

Michael struggled against my arms, freeing himself from my embrace. "Well, I've never laid eyes on him before. Who is this guy, Ellie?" He sounded angry and scared.

I didn't answer Michael. I knew that words could never be as powerful as images. I knew that Michael needed to see Rafe as he really was and hear the words as he really spoke them, to believe. And to follow.

I nodded to Rafe that the moment had come. As he had earlier, Rafe shook himself the tiniest bit. The movement released a haze of shimmering particles, almost like a golden dust. As it dispersed into the air, the rumpled teenage Rafe disappeared, only to be replaced by the ethereal Raphael.

Michael was frozen. Rafe did not fill the void with words; he awaited my lead. I knew I had to answer the question I'd purposely left unanswered before.

"Michael, Rafe is an angel. Not the fallen kind."

TWENTY-ONE

It was the first time I'd seen Michael rendered speechless.

I mustered up my courage, and said, "Michael, I know this is hard for you. To trust another being after everything that happened with Ezekiel. I assure you that Rafe is no Ezekiel, and his intentions are true."

I paused, allowing for Michael's reaction. He gave no response. Instead, he watched me silently, judging my every phrase and gesture. It seemed that his verdict still hung in the balance.

"Rafe risked everything to visit us. His kind"—I hesitated to use the term "angel" for some reason—"aren't meant to have contact with those on earth. They aren't supposed to interfere in any way with our free will. Here, the stakes are so high that Rafe chose to jeopardize his own well-being to help us with our destiny."

Michael still didn't say anything. I looked over at Rafe helplessly.

Rafe took over. "Ellspeth is telling you the truth, Michael. I've broken so many rules by offering my help. But I know that the earth and everyone on it will suffer if I don't assist you. So I've chosen to defy God's rules."

Michael raised an eyebrow at the mention of God and defying Him. Yet he didn't comment. He needed more persuasion, it seemed.

"To prove to you that I'm on your side, I'm going to share some of His secrets with you and Ellie. Secrets that will help you defeat the fallen and stop the end they crave," Rafe said.

It was my turn to listen. Since the moment Rafe had revealed his true nature to me on the street back in town, I had been waiting for more disclosures. Even though, after his story about the original two hundred angels and their punishments for revealing His secrets, I was surprised that he decided to risk God's wrath and divulge a few to us. No matter his assurances that God wouldn't punish him for helping us despite the prohibition.

"From Ellspeth, I learned that Ruth has pieced together some basic understanding of the end times. She told you that there are seven signs—seven events, or seals, as they are sometimes called—that will occur before the final day. Six of these events remain; the first sign, the earthquakes, has already happened. You will both need a much deeper understanding of the end days in order to stop the other signs. I've decided to share some of the missing pieces with you, although He has forbidden it."

Rafe's expression turned sorrowful at the mention of Him. I hadn't thought through how difficult on an emotional level it must be for an angel to disobey God. I felt immensely grateful to Rafe, even more than when he'd rescued me from Kael.

Rafe continued. "What Ruth didn't tell you is that certain fallen angels are responsible for the seven apocalyptic events. She couldn't have shared that with you because no human being knows this. Of the one hundred and seventy-five Dark Fallen—unlike the Light Fallen, such as your parents, who seek grace—only a few are capable of triggering the signs. Fewer now, since you've killed Ezekiel. Together, you must destroy the remaining fallen to prevent the final catastrophe from occurring. If you don't, the end days will quickly follow."

It made sense. "To stop an event we must kill the fallen angels? Not try to stop the event itself?" I asked.

"Yes." He nodded. "That's how it works."

"Is each fallen responsible only for one specific sign? Or can any of the seven trigger any of the signs?" Now that I understood what we were meant to accomplish, I was bursting with questions.

"Each of the chosen fallen has the capacity to activate only one sign. Or two, in a particular instance. He or she can set off only the sign or signs tied to their special gift of knowledge."

"Their special gift?"

"Yes, God entrusted each of these particular fallen with particular knowledge, wisdom known only to that angel and Him. Each sign is tied to that angel's special knowledge. For example, He confided in Ezekiel insights about the earth and its geological structure, including the cause of earthquakes. So, when the end days arrived, Ezekiel was able to instigate the end-days sign of earthquakes."

"What are the names of the others? And what are their special areas?" I needed to know.

"The second fallen is called Kael. Because he was gifted with knowledge of agriculture and the physical health of humankind, his second and third seals are disease and hunger. The third is Barakel, whose fourth seal is economic depression because he was given knowledge of coin and currency. Rumiel is the fourth fallen, and her fifth seal is persecution of the believers, as God charged her with giving humankind limited training in His ways. The fifth fallen is known as Azaziel—I mentioned him earlier—and his sixth is seal is warfare. The sixth and final fallen is Samyaza. He is charged with the seventh seal, the creation of an end-days leader, because he was the leader of the fallen when they first came to earth."

"If God gave them these insights, why doesn't He stop them from triggering the signs?" It seemed easy.

Rafe smiled. "That isn't His plan, Ellspeth. This is a battle between good and evil—light and dark—and His plan is to allow the free will and prowess of the Elect One to prevail. One way or another."

His words stifled my questions for a brief moment, but I believed that answers alone could help me succeed. If He meant this to be a pitched battle of wills between me and a bunch of fallen angels, I wanted every advantage. I wanted goodness and light to prevail. I'd seen darkness all too vividly in the sick flashes I'd received from Ezekiel's mind.

I took a deep breath, and launched right back in. "What happens if one of the seals doesn't open because we destroy the angel who was supposed to trigger it before he fulfills his mission? Does that stop the whole process? Have we won?"

"Each fallen you manage to annihilate is one less devastating event visited upon the earth. By killing even one fallen, you lessen the environmental damage and human suffering that the signs bring. The sign won't happen, but the end-days clock will still tick. To stop the end times altogether, you must destroy the fallen responsible for the final sign."

"The fallen who'll bring forth an end-days leader."

"Yes. Samyaza will be grooming a leader to rule the earth after apocalyptic events have reshaped it."

"Who are they preparing to be this leader? Do you know?"

My question actually made Rafe laugh, like the old, human Rafe. "So many questions, Ellspeth. Even though the clock is ticking, we'll have time enough to answer them all. Not at once."

"Tell me this, at least. Was Ruth right about the second event? That this huge volcano off the coast of Greenland will erupt, causing a chain reaction of maybe two of the seven signs?"

"Yes, Ruth's right."

"How can we find the angel responsible for the volcanic eruption?"

Rafe's smile changed. It transformed from the charming, slightly mischievous smile of the teenage Rafe to a sad, aged one that could only belong to the angel Raphael. "Ellspeth, there's no longer any need to locate that fallen. He has already found you. The fallen have heard that the Elect One has surfaced, and one by one, they have started coming for you."

How could I be so thick? The reality dawned on me. "Oh my God. Kael. The one that tried to get me tonight.

He is the one responsible for the volcano."

"Yes, Ellspeth. I mentioned him before. His special area is disease and hunger—the signs that will stem from the volcano."

Disease and hunger. That was the suffering Kael told me we were going to alleviate. How stupid could I be?

Then the really bad news sank in. "I had the chance, and I didn't kill him. I blew it. I didn't stop the sign."

"You couldn't have slain Kael. You don't yet know how."

"And you couldn't kill him?"

"No. I could only make sure that he won't come after you again."

I started to launch into a bunch of questions about how you kill these fallen angels, when Michael interjected. Finally.

"What are you two talking about? Who is Kael? What happened tonight?"

I turned in surprise. I had been so engrossed with Rafe's disclosures that I'd kind of forgotten about Michael. At least he still cared enough to perk up when he heard I'd been attacked.

Before I could explain, Rafe spoke in his soothing angel tone. "Don't worry, Michael. Ellspeth is fine. The fallen won't attempt to kill her. As the Elect One, she's far too valuable alive."

Rafe's words sounded uncannily like Ezekiel's. I wanted to ask more, but Rafe wasn't done with Michael.

"I've disclosed a lot, Michael. I revealed secrets that He commanded me to keep, and I've done that so that you and Ellspeth can succeed. I need to know that you will prepare alongside Ellspeth so that you will both be ready when the time comes. I need to know that you will stand with her. You have a special purpose too."

Michael's eyes looked distrustful. I couldn't believe that he still harbored doubts about Rafe. About me, maybe. Didn't he understand the sacrifice that Rafe was making? How lost we'd be without Rafe's assistance? How could he not get that the apocalypse was imminent? Unless we stopped it.

"Oh yeah? What would that be?" Michael's tone was confrontational.

Michael had some nerve challenging an angel. I expected some form of biblical wrath at Michael's continued obstinacy, yet Rafe seemed unfazed.

"If I tell you the nature of your destined role, Michael, we risk that you won't be able to fulfill it. This is one secret that I have to keep. For everyone's sake."

I had a feeling that there was something Rafe wasn't telling us. And not for the reason he mentioned.

"Will you stand alongside Ellspeth?" Rafe persisted in his questioning.

Michael squared his shoulders and gazed directly at Rafe. "Yes, I will. I'll do it to protect Ellie. For no other reason."

I glanced over at Rafe. Was this the answer he sought? Would Michael's begrudging agreement suffice? I prayed that it would.

Rafe beamed, and said, "That's good enough. Let's begin."

TWENTY-TWO

When Rafe said "begin," he meant begin *right now.*

Without a word of explanation, Rafe reached for our hands and lifted me and Michael into the air. It felt weird to fly again, almost like a kid who just took the training wheels off her bike. I welcomed—no, needed—the security of Rafe's hand at first. Even though I felt shaky, I was elated that the waiting was over. We were finally taking action.

Once we cleared the treetops and steadied ourselves, Rafe let go of our hands. The crisp nighttime air made me feel alive again. Like I'd reclaimed the latent part of myself and become whole. My shoulder blades lifted and expanded for the flight, and I relished the sensation of the wind and sky on my limbs and face. For a brief, wonderful minute, I forgot about the end days.

Then I noticed that Rafe had left me and Michael in his wake. I streamlined my body in an effort to keep up with Rafe's incredibly swift pace. His motions were so precise and so efficient that I could not possibly catch up. He practically had to backpedal to fly alongside me and Michael.

Where were we going? I tried to track the landmarks on the ground. I ticked off my parents' house, our high school, even the old town church that used to creep me out with its circular window that stared out like some all-seeing eye. Still, I couldn't figure out our destination.

Within a few minutes, I spotted a familiar ring of fir trees. The circle of evergreens enclosed a private field. *Our* field. Why was Rafe bringing us here? Did he know it was our special place?

We lowered ourselves carefully to the ground. No one spoke a word until we stood together on the field's central mound.

"You're familiar with this place?" Rafe broke the silence.

"Yes," I answered. "Michael and I used to come here when I was learning to fly. He discovered it."

Rafe glanced over at Michael and nodded in approval. "Intuitively, you chose well. Although you couldn't possibly have known, this field is embedded with protections that shielded you somewhat from the fallen. The protections didn't entirely mask your fledging efforts with your powers—as you saw with Ezekiel—but they bought you considerable time. I'm hoping that it will offer us similar protection while we train."

"How is it possible that Michael stumbled across a field containing these 'protections?' That's too incredible to be a coincidence."

"Ellspeth, your parents lived in Tillinghast in the sixteen hundreds, right after they decided to try for redemption. At that time, the Dark Fallen were trying to persuade them and the other Light Fallen to return, through some rather unpleasant means. Your parents needed a place where they could be safe. They created this haven."

I recalled my conversation with my parents when they revealed their true natures, and their smiles reminiscing on their "happy times" in Tillinghast. They made their disclosure before I went to Boston, of course. Before they tried to make me forget all over again.

I choked up a bit as I thought about all the sacrifices my parents had made for humankind and me. I felt guilty about being so mad at them lately. "My parents created this place as a sanctuary nearly four hundred years ago?"

"Yes. When Michael found it, he probably sensed it was a refuge." Rafe nodded again in Michael's direction. I think he was trying to reassure him, offer another olive branch. Michael had been very quiet during this whole exchange. I could tell that a part of him was still watching and weighing.

As I stared from one to the other, they seemed so

different. Rafe was dark where Michael was light, in the hair and eyes. Rafe's strength was obvious and burly, while Michael's force was lean and compact. Rafe retained his lightness and humor, as Michael had become extra serious. Yet, despite all their disparities, they had one powerful quality in common—the desire to protect me.

I returned to the conversation. Rafe had mentioned my parents. The question begged to be asked.

"Rafe, is it time to tell our parents that we know who we are?"

He paused, considering the question. "Not yet, Ellspeth."

"Why not? Hiding our powers and pretending hasn't stopped the end days from proceeding. What is there to gain by keeping them in the dark?"

"Feigning ignorance might not stop the opening of the seven seals, but it will protect your parents for a little while. Once you tell your parents what you know, they will summon the other Light Fallen. The Dark Fallen will perceive it as a call to battle. The end will hasten, and we'll lose this opportunity to prepare you. Also"—Rafe hesitated a second—"your parents won't survive. Don't forget that they are mortal."

At the mention of my parents' mortality, the tears threatened to reappear, but I willed them away and said, "Surely our parents could restrain themselves from summoning the Light Fallen? So that Michael and I could have time to prepare? That way, we could loop them in but still get what we need." I suddenly had an urge to have my parents at my side.

"It isn't so simple, Ellspeth. Centuries ago, the Light Fallen vowed to align for the end-days battle as soon as it surfaced. The agreement leaves no room for waiting."

"So we have to go on with this charade," I said. I hated lying to them, but if it bought our parents more time, I would put on an Academy Award–level performance.

"For now, you must." Rafe gestured around the field and changed the subject. "This is where we'll train. Every night, until it's time."

Michael finally perked up. "This is where you'll teach us how to crush them, right?"

Rafe ignored Michael's show of bravado, and stated the blunt facts. "Neither you nor Ellspeth will ever overpower them. Remember, their nature is pure angel, while yours is only half. So, they have double the power you have. If you can fly fast, they can fly twice as fast, for example. Still, you bear tremendous strength and gifts within your bodies, and used wisely, you'll be able to destroy the fallen before the final seal is broken. Plus, your humanity has its own unique gifts."

"If we can't overpower them, how will we kill them?"

Michael persisted impatiently. It seemed that he wanted to bypass the training and get right to the murder part.

"Do you know how you were able to kill Ezekiel? Your father?"

I watched Michael's bullishness ratchet down a notch at Rafe's reminder that Ezekiel was actually his father. Michael said quietly, "I pushed him into a steel pole."

Rafe responded even more quietly. He understood that the destruction of Ezekiel had taken a private toll on Michael, and empathy imbued Rafe's voice. "That alone wouldn't have killed him, Michael. The fallen are immortal, except for one flaw."

Suddenly the words spoken by Tamiel—the angel sent to Boston by my parents to help us—came back to me. "Only one with Ezekiel's blood in his veins can destroy him," I blurted out.

Rafe faced me. "Yes, Ellspeth. Only the *Nephilim* who has the fallen's blood in his or her veins can destroy him."

So we needed to have our target fallen angel's blood coursing through our veins to slay him. How would we go about that? "Ezekiel was Michael's father. That's how Michael had Ezekiel's blood in his veins. We cannot possibly be the children of *all* the five remaining fallen angels responsible for the signs. How can we get their blood in our veins?"

As the question left my mouth, a memory returned to me. In Boston, Michael told me that Ezekiel was able to track him because Ezekiel's blood ran in Michael's veins, and that Ezekiel could track me for the same reason. The reason that Ezekiel's blood ran in my veins was that I had tasted Michael's blood. Suddenly, I understood what we needed to do in order to kill the fallen, and Rafe watched my face as it all became clear.

I answered my own question. "We have to spill their blood and drink it."

Michael looked over at me, horrified and disgusted. "That can't be right."

Very calmly and very plainly, Rafe said, "Ellspeth is right. You must draw blood from the fallen and make it your own, before delivering the final blow. You need only taste the fallen's blood to make it one with yours. I will teach you how to do it. That way, you can destroy the fallen responsible for the end days before it's too late."

Twenty-three

I thought we'd get a breather after that first night. That maybe we'd spend the next few evenings learning more about Nephilim history and the prophecy. That we'd launch into training after some rest and reflection.

After all, I had a million questions, even more than I'd already deluged Rafe with. I yearned for an understanding of how we came into being; who our birth parents were; the scope of our powers; the details of the prophecy; the nature and endgame of these fallen; how we'd find them; what they wanted from us; and, maybe most of all, what would happen if we failed. The list was endless, and the deeper I dug, the more questions I had. I longed for a tutorial at the feet of an angel, and I prayed I'd get one.

I didn't. There were no academic lectures on Rafe's agenda on Saturday and Sunday nights. There were no elaborate speeches scheduled for the late night hours. There was only grueling physical instruction—torture, actually.

Apparently, Michael and I needed to hone our bodily skills more than we needed to sharpen our angelic knowledge. Me especially.

"Up," Rafe barked at us on Sunday night, after watching Michael and me race around the field and perform all sorts of exercises for nearly an hour.

Michael and I glanced at each other in confusion, and then back at Rafe. "We're already up."

"Not in the air, you're not."

Up Rafe flew, and up we went. As we penetrated the lower cloud cover, Rafe yelled out the names of the specific cloud types. He pointed out how the different layers felt on our skin and hair and arms, and showed us how to use that knowledge to gauge the weather and alter our speed accordingly. He also demonstrated how we could use those same clouds as camouflage in the sky. His instruction reminded me of a passage from the Book of Enoch where the humans first learned His mysteries at the behest of an angel.

As we rushed through the last cloud layer straight into the upper atmosphere, Rafe shouted back at us, "The fallen are stronger than you, so you'll have to use all the nuances of your natures to outmaneuver them. No offense, Ellspeth, but you'll never outrun them on the ground. You're too slow and too"—I could almost hear Rafe suppress a laugh—"too intellectual."

Knowing full well that Rafe actually meant clumsy, I retorted, "Are you sure you'd like me to be the Elect One?"

"*He* chose you, Ellspeth. Not me," he answered with that old, impish grin.

That shut me up. I hadn't given much thought to being handpicked by *Him*. Why He picked me immediately became the number one question on my growing list.

I heard Rafe's voice through the wind whipping by my ears. "We'll have to practice in the skies, where we might get you an advantage. Michael, since I need you by Ellspeth's side, you'll have to be airborne as well."

Rafe instructed us to stay in the air above the ring of fir trees, to hide the use of our powers. The space was relatively small, but it became amazingly large when you used it vertically. We followed his orders to race to the heavens and then plummet downward, to make one-hundred-and-eighty-degree turns, to stop on a dime, and to pivot and swoop in directions I didn't even know existed. All the while Rafe watched and assessed.

Michael was a natural at whatever feat Rafe asked him to perform. In awe, I watched Michael plunge to the earth with such force I nearly screamed in fear for his life, only to have him back at my side before I blinked. As nimble and athletic as he was on the football field, it was nothing compared to his grace and agility in the sky.

My skills were a different matter.

After one particularly harrowing nosedive, Rafe flew to my side and placed his hands on my shoulders. "Let's try that again. I'll fly along with you."

I got in position, thousands of feet from the ground, and faced downward. Rafe aligned his body with mine, shoulder to shoulder, chest to chest. Despite the locale and despite the proximity of Michael, it felt surprisingly intimate.

He whispered in my ear, "Dive."

Stretching out my arms as if I were about to leap off a board into a swimming pool, I dove headlong. As I gained momentum, Rafe corrected my position, broadening my shoulders, lengthening my arms, and narrowing the gap between my ankles. I felt myself flying faster than ever before, and enjoying it more than ever before.

Almost too much. I forgot to stop.

Fortunately, in the split second before impact, Rafe swung my legs down under me, and ordered, "Hover!"

Amazingly, I floated down the remaining five feet. I didn't need to grind to a halt or allow myself a hundred feet to put on the brakes. Rafe taught me that the exercise of my powers could be simple.

Time and again, Rafe flew to my side and adjusted my posture or uttered some small tip. By the time I started to see the glimmer of sun in the horizon, I'd mastered most of the skills Rafe set out for us. I'd never match Michael's stellar performance, but at least I felt like I could hold my own. I was utterly exhausted by my efforts.

We descended to earth, and joined Rafe on the central mound. He issued some instructions about our daytime behavior and our plans to meet the following evening. Before dawn broke, we were about to go our separate ways when Michael piped up. He had been so quiet all night— seemingly focused on impressing Rafe with his aerial tactics—that I was shocked when he asked one of the questions ringing in my head all night.

"Why are you teaching us all this stuff? So we can be strong enough to collect their blood and drink it"—Michael shuddered at the very thought—"before killing them?"

"That is certainly one reason," Rafe responded, ever careful and enigmatic in his answers.

"What is another reason?" Michael pushed back. I saw that he didn't like Rafe's evasiveness one bit, angel or not.

"To avoid Ellspeth's capture. As I said before, the fallen won't kill her. They need her."

For some reason, that idea scared me more than if he'd said they desperately wanted to murder me. Hesitantly, I asked, "What is it that they want from me?"

"The fallen want you to stand by their side at the end. They want to convince you of their views—that they were right to disobey Him in the beginning and that they've been justified in defying Him ever since. They will use all methods at their disposal to do so." He grew uncommonly quiet. "And they have many powerful methods of persuasion."

"Like what?" I asked.

"They will prey upon your main weakness. Your humanity."

"Like Kael tried to do to me? By telling me that together we could lessen disease and hunger for humankind?"

"Yes. And the means by which they'll prey on your humanity will usually tie to the seal that they're supposed to unlock."

"And if that doesn't work?" I wanted to know what Kael would've tried next.

"They might try something more overt, like threatening people around you," Rafe answered. I remembered that Tamiel had said something like this about Ezekiel.

"What if they can't persuade her?" Michael asked.

"And they won't," I said. I thought that nothing could convince me.

"Then they'll trigger their sign anyway. But they'll let Ellspeth live. If they can't sway her, they'll want one of their kind to succeed in persuading her to the side of the fallen. Whoever is responsible for the next sign will try next. The fallen won't want Ellie to side against them at the very end."

"Why? Why do they care if I believe them or not?" It didn't make sense to me.

"Because the prophecy says that, when the seventh seal is broken and the end days are upon us, the Elect One will judge all earthly beings. With you at their side, they believe that you will judge their decisions and their reign here on earth to be fair."

"Me? Who would ever believe me to be capable of judging everyone?"

"He does, Ellspeth."

There was that *He* again. "So basically, the fallen want me at their side, so I can rig the jury for them?"

"Ellspeth, the fallen no longer want to fall."

TWENTY-FOUR

As I lay my head down on my enticingly soft pillow on Sunday night, really Monday morning, I glanced over at the clock. It read 5:48. I did a quick calculation and realized that I'd have only seventy-six minutes of sleep before the alarm rang for school.

I figured it wasn't even worth nodding off for those scant minutes; past experience taught me that sometimes a little sleep was worse than none at all. It left me groggy and ill-tempered. So I lay there, watching the clock change: 5:49 and 5:50. I remembered the clock hitting 5:51 before my mom shook me awake for school at 7:04. She'd never had to do that before.

After my mom left my room, I lifted off my sheets and lowered myself from my high sleigh bed to the floor. Every single muscle in my body ached. No, screamed in pain. What had Rafe done to me? How did he expect me to fight off the fallen in this condition?

Hobbling down the hallway to the bathroom, I prayed that a hot shower and some ibuprofen would take the edge off the agony. I allowed myself a few extra minutes in the steam, and then eased myself out of the shower and into my clothes. My muscles didn't shriek, at least. Maybe I'd make it through the school day, although I wasn't too optimistic about another evening of Rafe's instruction.

When I finally made it down the stairs, I found my mom at the kitchen counter, preparing my usual wheat toast and raspberry jam. Hiding my pain, I chatted with her about the day ahead, as we always did. For the first time since I returned from Boston, it wasn't hard to make pleasant small talk with her. The anger I felt at my parents' deceptions had subsided, replaced by empathy. Rafe had helped me to better understand what they'd risked to raise me in what they thought was necessary ignorance.

A honk from Michael's car interrupted our innocuous conversation. I slung my bag over my shoulder and said good-bye to my mom. A sudden compulsion overcame me, and I spun around and hugged her. No matter what—angel or mortal, fallen or redeemed, birth or adoptive—she was my mom, first and foremost. Who knew when I would next have the chance to embrace her or my dad? I needed to cherish every last second with them.

"Is everything all right, dearest?" my mom asked as

I broke away and headed toward the door. She looked concerned.

"Of course," I said, with the brightest smile I could manage. "Why wouldn't everything be all right?" Then I waved good-bye.

I eased myself into Michael's idling Prius. As I leaned over to give him a kiss, I noticed dark circles under his eyes and a pale sheen to his skin. I'd never seen him looking so exhausted.

We had shared many near-sleepless evenings together, but nothing like the last couple of nights. We were accustomed to leisurely flights, followed by long hours of intimacy, not relentless physical torment. With the prospect of more tonight.

My attempts at conversation—of the lighthearted variety recommended by Rafe for any talk outside our protected field—were met by little more than grunts, and I stopped trying after a few minutes. We hadn't had much chance to talk alone over the weekend and I figured he was still mad at me for springing Rafe on him. Although he didn't have much right to be angry. Normally, I'd be upset by his coldness, but today, I was so tired myself that I didn't care. It was a relief to ride to school in silence. Anyway, I felt calmer being near him, regardless of his gruffness.

I barely made it through the day with my facade intact.

Normalcy seemed so futile in the face of the coming Armageddon. Only Rafe's reminder of the importance of appearances kept my eyes from closing during Miss Taunton's droning on about Edith Wharton. Only his warning against confiding anything to Ruth—for her own protection, he said, as she was already vulnerable—kept me from divulging the latest developments to her over lunch. Instead I listened to forty minutes' worth of Jamie stories, while struggling to keep my eyes open.

My contact with Michael throughout the day was minimal. Unusually so. Except for a brief meeting at my locker before he headed off to football practice—God knows how he'd manage to make it through Coach Samuel's notorious drills—I hardly saw him. Truly, all I could think about was an after-school nap, and I guessed he felt the same.

I awoke from it, feeling refreshed and healed. Almost magically so. I had a pleasant dinner with my parents, in which we laughed over some e-mails from a Kenyan colleague from last summer. As we did the dishes together, I couldn't stop thinking about the story Rafe had told me about the beginning, about all they had sacrificed to regain grace, about all the love and caring they'd given me. After we finished, I hugged them tightly, and excused myself to go upstairs for homework and bed. The entire evening felt like the beginnings of good-bye, and I had to keep my emotions under wraps. For their protection.

I settled into my bedroom, and awaited Rafe.

Over the weekend, Rafe had explained that he didn't want Michael or me to venture to the field alone. He would be watching over us during the day to ensure that the exercise of our powers hadn't lured any more fallen. However, he said, it was harder to monitor them—and us—at night. Hence the escort.

Even though I expected him and even though I watched his arrival on Saturday and Sunday nights, the sight of Rafe's chocolate hair and inky eyes in the window still startled me. I'd grown used to Michael's pale hair and green eyes looming outside my windowsill. Resorting to my old tricks, I eased the creaky old window up, and slid out into the night. Fingers crossed that my parents didn't hear, although for very different reasons than before.

As Rafe explained that he'd already taken Michael to the field, I took his hand, and we lifted off into the pitch-black sky. Even though we'd done nothing untoward, the act seemed very personal to me.

As we coasted over Tillinghast's little downtown and the university campus, I tried to keep my focus on the familiar landmarks or Rafe's tutorial on the types of winds through which we were flying. Yet I couldn't stop some of those initial feelings I'd experienced with Rafe from creeping in.

Despite the fact that the angelic Raphael had replaced the human Rafe, and had become a mentor to me in the process, the two Rafes were very similar. They both shared a unique blend of strength and sensitivity, bursts of humor, and a core faith in humankind that was very attractive.

Hands still locked, Rafe and I landed on the field. As we alighted, I watched Michael study me and Rafe, our hands in particular. The scrutiny made me uncomfortable, and I raced over to Michael's side. Very pointedly, Michael grabbed me for a rough embrace and enveloping kiss. The affection seemed to have little to do with me; he seemed to be sending a message to Rafe. Because, as soon as Rafe looked away, Michael abruptly let go of me.

Rafe seemed impervious to the little display.

"Ellspeth and Michael, tonight we will focus on weaponry." Rafe gestured around the field. "I've assembled a fair representation of readily available armaments."

We looked at the items spread across the springy grass. Nestled in among the heather, tufts of autumn wildflowers, and green ground cover was an incongruous array of gleaming arms. Axes, knives, spears, and swords sat alongside a host of weapons I'd never seen before. Rafe had a very strange sense of the average, everyday human world if he deemed these items to be "readily available armaments."

"Select one and follow me into the skies. That is where

your war will be waged, so we should practice there."

I reached for a golden-handled sword with a medium-size blade—it seemed the most manageable of the daunting lot—and soared into the chilly night air. Michael and I hovered next to Rafe as he displayed some basic sword skills, like thrusts and parries. Then he showed us how to injure the fallen enough to draw blood, not kill. The moves appeared effortless in Rafe's capable hands, but I knew he made it look deceptively easy.

As Rafe conducted his demonstration, he advised, "Your initial goal is to wound, not kill. Never forget that you must draw and ingest the fallen's blood first—and only then attempt destruction. Otherwise, the fallen's wound will heal almost immediately, and you will be very close to a very angry angel."

Rafe's comments made me wonder about my own recuperative powers. I'd healed quickly, despite last night's exertions. "Do our wounds heal fast too?"

"Faster than a normal human's, although not as fast as a full angel's. Remember what I told you yesterday. Your power is half theirs."

"Does that mean we are physically less vulnerable than a normal human?" I quickly reviewed my past medical and physical history. I was almost never sick, and I couldn't remember a single injury of any sort. Not even the typical childhood breaks and cuts requiring the emergency room.

"Yes." Rafe could see where I was going with my line of questioning. "But you are not immortal, Ellspeth. Only full angels never die."

"Fallen and full angels, like you?"

"The fallen and full angels have the same powers, the same immortality. The primary difference is that the fallen cannot enter heaven, their true home," Rafe answered. Then, tutorial over, he nodded to Michael. "You first. Do you think you can imitate me?"

Michael smiled a bit cockily. "I think I can give it a shot."

I watched as Michael reproduced Rafe's moves almost exactly. Even though I was annoyed with his arrogance, especially toward Rafe, he had every reason to be confident. Michael was a natural.

When Michael finished, he returned to his position next to me and Rafe. His cheeks were flushed from the exertions despite the coldness of the air, and he looked exhilarated from performing so expertly.

Rafe turned to me and said the words I dreaded: "Ellspeth, you're next."

I tried. Really, I did. But the blade weighed heavy in my hand, and my thrusts and parries felt more like the limp workings of an overcooked noodle. It was embarrassing to display my awkwardness in its full glory before Rafe and Michael, two of the most agile beings that I'd ever encountered.

My discomfort worsened when I noticed that Michael appeared oddly pleased by my struggles. In fact, he looked downright smug at besting me in the training. Hadn't Ezekiel said Michael was meant "to be knight to his lady?" There was no evidence of chivalry on Michael's face.

As usual, Rafe rushed to my side to help me. As he had the night before, he corrected my stance, changed my grip, and showed me how to brandish the sword with the right timing. After several tries, I got the hang of it. Still, I didn't think I'd stand a chance against a determined fallen. And Rafe seemed to agree.

"Michael, you'll do well in hand-to-hand combat against any of the fallen. Ellspeth"—Rafe paused, as if weighing whether to state the obvious. "I have serious concerns should you find yourself in battle. For Ellspeth's sake, I'm going to train you both in one more weapon for your arsenal, even though I'm reluctant to do so. You must use this weapon only when you have absolutely no other recourse, because summoning the weapon and using it will weaken you tremendously. If you miss your mark, you'll be so weak that you'll be an easy victim for the fallen. And never, ever use it alone. Only use it when the other is present. Because if either of you miscalculate, the other must have your back."

"What is this weapon?" Michael asked, ever eager when it came to all things battle.

Rafe backed away from us, about a hundred feet. He extended his arm, stretched out his fingers, and closed his eyes. From his fingertips emanated a stream of light, not unlike the arcs of light that radiated from our backs during flight. Almost laserlike in its intensity, the light soon formed a shape. It became a blade, resembling the flaming swords I'd seen in many Renaissance paintings of angels.

"This is the sword of fire, our purest weapon. It is a weapon of the mind and soul—rather than the body. You must concentrate with the core of your being to summon it."

Rafe stood us side by side. Rather than having us attempt the summoning one after the other, he wanted us to try it simultaneously. Perhaps he sensed that Michael's prowess was intimidating me.

"Close your eyes. Imagine the blade. Call to it," Rafe whispered.

At first, I felt nothing but stupid. Calling to a nonexistent blade? Come on. I screwed my eyes shut and concentrated as hard as I thought I could. Nothing happened.

When I opened them, Rafe was staring at me with a bemused expression.

"Ellspeth, you've got to do more than scrunch up your

eyebrows to make the sword of fire. You must believe in yourself to summon the blade. Believe that God chose you to be the Elect One. Believe that you have within you the divine power to fulfill that role. Believe that the power can be harnessed and shaped into a weapon of light and strength. Repeat these truths to yourself as you concentrate. Now, try again," he ordered, and glanced over at Michael. "Both of you."

I still felt stupid. Regardless, I did as Rafe requested. I repeated to myself his "truths," although they didn't seem all that self-evident to me. I told myself that I had been selected by Him, whoever He was, for this job, that I had power enough to fashion a weapon of light. I mouthed the words over and over.

Soon I experienced deep warmth inside my body. It traveled down my arm until it grew almost unbearable in intensity. The heat seemed to ignite and then burst forth from my fingertips. I opened my eyes to witness a perfect blade of light streaming from my hand. I couldn't believe that I had done it.

"Excellent, Ellspeth." Rafe grinned, pleased at his star pupil. For once.

I looked over at Michael, triumphant and excited. Finally, I had something to offer him in the way of assistance against our pursuers. I hoped that that he'd be relieved that I could finally help when the fallen came. I thought that he'd be delighted, even.

But there he stood, with only a weak, blue light trickling from his palm, looking none too pleased by my success.

Michael stormed off into the clouds. Leaving Rafe behind, I flew after him.

"Why are you acting this way, Michael?" I yelled, hoping that he could hear me above the howl of the wind.

He didn't slow his pace at all. I thought that maybe he didn't reduce his speed because he couldn't hear my cry. Without warning, he pivoted toward me. A scowl loomed upon his face.

"You always have to be the Elect One, don't you?" he shouted back at me.

"What do you mean?" I had suspected that Michael felt that way, but it hurt hearing the words spoken. And his remark was totally unwarranted. I had never lorded over him the pronouncement about the Elect One. How could I, when I found it hard to believe myself? When I relied on Michael as my equal partner in all things? When I thought of him as my love and soul mate? When I didn't even want to be the Elect One?

"The sword of fire, Ellie. You summoned up the 'purest weapon' perfectly, didn't you?" Michael answered my question literally, although we both knew there was much,

much more to his comment.

"You are being completely unfair, Michael. It's not like I even want to be the Elect One. You'd be a million times better for the job. You're a better fighter; you're faster and more agile than me. And you're a heck of a lot braver. I'd love to hand over the role to you, but I can't. Anyway, about this ridiculous sword of fire you're so mad about, you are better at a hundred things, Michael. I happen to be able to do this one thing. I thought you'd be happy that I could help out for once, instead of being a clumsy liability."

"How could the Elect One ever be a clumsy liability?" He didn't say the "Elect One" nicely. He said it like a curse.

"Look, Michael, they may call me the Elect One, but you and I both know that I'm just a girl who's trying to figure it out. And I thought I was figuring it out with you."

His expression softened, and he reached for me. "I know, Ellie. I'm sorry. It's hard sometimes to play the knight to your Elect One."

TWENTY-FIVE

The next morning, the end-days clock began to tick within me. I don't know what caused this shift, yet with every minute and hour that passed, I sensed the end of time growing closer. I realized that I couldn't waste a second of what remained.

I didn't know when the fallen would come for us again. Every moment needed to be dedicated to our preparation. We needed to be armed and ready—physically and mentally—so that we could annihilate them before they unleashed the six remaining signs. Or God knows what would follow. Rafe hadn't yet divulged to us what failure would look like.

Yet we couldn't spend every moment practicing with Rafe. He had insisted that we maintain our facades to buy us this tiny window for training, and to protect our parents as best we could. That day, I rushed through my classes and homework, knowing they were pointless if Michael and I didn't succeed. I hurried through my after-school coffee with Ruth. I even hastened through my limited time alone with Michael, no great sacrifice given our tiff and his ongoing self-absorption and continued focus on football.

I told myself there would be time enough to deal with Michael "after"—should there be an "after." I awoke from my nap feeling more and more confident in my role as the Elect One, and found it easier to stave off the roller coaster of emotions that Michael's inconsistent behavior yielded. And focus on the battle coming.

The only moments that day I tried to decelerate were those with my parents. For once, I cherished my mom's relentless chatter over breakfast. For maybe the first time, I appreciated my dad's dated jokes at dinnertime, laughing heartily, much to his surprise and delight. Who knew when—or if—those moments would come again?

I waited until I reached the sky over our protected field to truly come alive. Rafe began with a lesson in reading the stars, so that we could always keep our bearings as we fought in a vertical terrain. As he finished, however, Rafe must have sensed the divide between Michael and me. Rather than address the rift head-on, Rafe separated us for the training. Maybe he thought we'd learn better, and like each other more, with some distance.

Rafe taught Michael some advanced flying techniques

and sword skills—talents way beyond me—while I watched patiently. I was amazed by Michael's performance. Even though it had only been five days since we started training with Rafe, Michael's abilities had grown exponentially under Rafe's tutelage, so much that he matched Rafe move for move. It was like he'd been waiting for the training to bloom.

After Rafe set up Michael with a few sequences to practice, he flew over to me. "Ready?"

"What tricks do you have up your sleeve for me today?" I was ready and willing for whatever torture Rafe dished out, all the while praying that the evening's fare was more of the mental variety than the physical. I performed much better with a conjured sword than a steel one.

He humored me with a half smile, and then he was down to business. Apparently, there wasn't enough time left even for lame jokes. "Ellspeth, I've told you before that the fallen will try to use their considerable powers of persuasion on you."

"Yeah, they're desperate to have me adopt their slanted worldview. That it's all right to create their own race in defiance of Him. I get it."

"We can't let that happen. If it does, we've lost the war. No matter how fast Michael can fly or how well he can fight."

"I need to learn how to prevent the fallen from influencing my thoughts." It wasn't a question. "I can't let happen what almost happened with Kael."

"Exactly." Rafe paused for a moment, and then said, "I think you intuitively know how to stop their efforts. We need only to hone the skill."

"I'm not sure what 'skill' you're talking about."

"Did you notice that you were able to exercise your own will with Ezekiel, while others were more susceptible to Ezekiel's call?"

Rafe didn't need to spell it out. By "others," he meant Michael. "Yes."

"Do you remember how you did it?"

Shutting my eyes, I conjured up the unpleasant memories of Ezekiel trying to bend my will that awful night on Ransom Beach. I recalled that—instinctively and immediately—I had fashioned a mental shield of sorts against him. It had staved him off.

"I think so," I answered hesitantly.

"Let's try it again here. Use all your mental and physical might to fly toward Michael. I'll try to hold you back, through your thoughts."

I nodded my assent, and located Michael's position in the skies. Streamlining my body and broadening my shoulders as Rafe had taught me, I hurled myself into the clouds.

Through the vaporous cover, Michael grew more distinct as I neared him. As I was about to make contact, I felt myself jerked back as if someone had grabbed my shoulders with all his strength.

I feigned compliance, the same way I had with Ezekiel, and stopped my attempt to reach Michael. In that split second, I sensed Rafe slacken his efforts ever so slightly. That provided me with the tiny opening to build what felt like a fortress around my mind. Now defended against Rafe, I reasserted my own will and bashed right into Michael's arms.

Arms wrapped around me, Michael stared at me with his pale green eyes. Spontaneously, we smiled at each other as if nothing had happened—not his betrayal with Ezekiel, not the travails in Boston, not the fights and misunderstandings upon our return to Tillinghast, and not the momentous weight of learning who and what we were. We smiled at each other as we had that first day in the hallways of Tillinghast Upper School, when we were just Ellie and Michael. It was these moments that reminded me of what we really meant to each other.

Rafe appeared.

"I don't think we need to practice that maneuver again, Ellspeth. You have it down."

"Maneuver?" Michael asked. He looked confused, not

to mention crestfallen.

"Ellspeth proved that she can hold her own against the fallen's formidable persuasive powers. Mentally, anyway."

Michael thought that I'd flown over simply to be with him. His arms suddenly slackened, and I started to plummet through the skies. Rafe's sturdy hand grabbed me before I spiraled out of control.

"I think you and Michael are ready," Rafe announced, once I'd steadied myself and caught my breath.

"Ready for what?" Michael asked, his voice gruff.

"Ready to learn a skill that only a few angels possess."

"I thought we were already doing that. You know, killing the fallen."

Rafe ignored him. "We're going to channel our internal energies so that we can fly a great distance in a mere instant."

"How do we do that?" Michael asked, incredulous at the possibility of this new power. And eager.

"First, close your eyes. You imagine your destination. The way it looks, the way it sounds, even the way it smells. Every brick in the building's walls, every waft of cooking in the air, every conversation you overheard, every little nuance that you can remember about the place."

"What if you've never been to the place before?" I interrupted.

Rafe smiled. Sometimes my endless questions amused him. "You conjure up the details as best you can. Invent them if necessary. It helps if you're accurate. It's not absolutely critical, though. As long as your intention is true."

"Then what?"

"You focus your entire being on this place. Each and every cell in your body. Then you breathe and let go."

"And you're there? Just like that?" Michael asked. He couldn't believe that something so amazing could be so easy.

"Projection only sounds simple. The description is deceptive. It actually requires lots of concentration." Rafe stretched out his hands. "Shall we try? Don't worry about the destination this first time, I'll take the lead."

Leave the safety of the field? Wouldn't that be like broadcasting our powers to the fallen? Why was Rafe suggesting we take such a dangerous risk? "Aren't you worried about what might happen if we exercise our powers outside the field?"

Rafe looked over at me, and I thought I saw sadness in his dark eyes. "Not anymore, Ellspeth."

Before I had a chance to ask him what he meant, we linked hands.

TWENTY-SIX

A vortex engulfed me. It felt like a tornado of light instead of wind. It was so blinding I shut my eyes, and clung to Rafe's and Michael's hands.

When the light finally ceased and I dared to look, I stared at a chorus of angels. They soared through an azure sky dotted with vibrant white clouds. These angels were not of the cherubic, Valentine-card variety. They were muscular and fierce. Some carried trumpets, while others bore items of a more peculiar nature, like a ladder or a wheel. All moved with distinct purpose.

Had I died and gone to heaven?

I allowed my vision to focus in the otherwise dim light. No, this place was familiar. I'd been here before, with my parents. The angels and the clouds and the creatures among them were not real. In fact, they were exquisite paintings—masterpieces—that decorated every single surface of a structure that resembled the interior of a treasure chest.

Suddenly it dawned on me. It was the Sistine Chapel.

Michael asked, "Where the hell are we, Rafe?"

"Doesn't it look familiar to you, Michael?"

He loosened his grip on my hand and strolled around. "It looks like we've stepped into a page of an art history textbook."

"That isn't too far off the mark. You are in Rome, at the Vatican. This is the—"

"Sistine Chapel." Michael got it. "Wow, you were able to transport us here by channeling your energy."

"Yes."

"Can you teach us to do this projection thing?" Michael wasn't awed by the locale. He didn't even seem interested in why Rafe had selected this place. It was all about the new skill for him.

"Yes. I'll show you how to do it on our return home to Tillinghast."

Maybe Michael didn't care, but I needed to know why this place, of all the places in the world. For Rafe did nothing without a very clear purpose. "Why did you bring us here, Rafe?"

"Why the Sistine Chapel?"

"Yes."

"Isn't it reason enough that it is one of the most sacred places in the world, famous for its architecture and the paintings by Michelangelo?"

"No, Rafe. I don't think of you as a tour guide or an art history buff."

He laughed. Not a celestial sound but a very human laugh. "You've gotten to know me well, Ellspeth. I have my reasons."

"Given that the clock is ticking, do you think you might share them with us?" For once, I didn't care if I sounded acerbic or challenging. The time was at hand, and it demanded answers.

Rafe pulled us to the very center of the Sistine Chapel. He directed our gaze to the ceiling this time, pointing to the iconic image of God creating Adam through a single touch of His hand. We rose to see it up close. The painting was so powerful—so real—that I could almost feel the current of life passing from God to Adam.

"This is the God I know well. A loving God. One who can be quick to judge, yet one who is quick to forgive. A God who gives second chances. This is the force that courses through you both. This is the force that should guide the end."

Taking me and Michael firmly by the hands, Rafe led us downward. We swooped behind an iron grate guarding an altar in one corner of the room, so we could better see the enormous painting behind the altar.

"This is Michelangelo's masterpiece, *The Last Judgment*. I think it's the most accurate rendering of the end days by the hand of a human. It shows the souls of humanity rising and descending to their fates—after the end days already happened—as judged by the Elect One, here depicted as Christ."

He pulled us closer to the painting. "This painting also contains a hidden message. Michelangelo encoded *The Last Judgment* with a message explicitly for you, Ellspeth."

I shook my head in disbelief. "Michelangelo hid a message in *The Last Judgment* for Ellspeth Faneuil? Centuries ago? Come on, Rafe."

"*The Last Judgment* is inspired by visions God sent to Michelangelo. Images that He wanted the Elect One to see, when the time was right. You're the Elect One. This is the time. Yes, Ellspeth, as impossible as it may seem, Michelangelo hid a message in *The Last Judgment* for you."

I shuddered. Somehow, the notion that the legendary Michelangelo painted an image for me—one imbedded with meaning, no less—made my mission all too overwhelmingly real.

"What is the message?"

"The message is for you, Ellspeth. Not me. Only the Elect One can decipher it. Why don't you see if you can figure it out?"

"I'm no art historian, Rafe."

"I don't think it's that kind of message, Ellspeth."

Rafe released our hands, and flew off alone to a far corner of the chapel. He seemed lost in his own thoughts, even a bit sad. Or perhaps he simply wanted to leave me to my project, with Michael as my helpmate. Who could discern the thought process of an angel? I was tired of trying.

With that, Michael and I were left alone. For a long few minutes, we hovered in front of the vast, immensely tall painting, taking in the vivid portraits of angels and demons and everything in between.

"Amazing, huh?" Michael commented.

I appreciated his attempt at small talk. It'd been a while since he'd made the effort. "I'll say. It's incredible being so close."

"Without all the crowds," Michael added.

I nodded. Suddenly, a figure toward the bottom of the painting caught my attention. It was the cowering figure of a man, enfolded by three snakelike demons. His face writhed in pain and terror as the demons dragged him downward. The image sent shivers up my spine.

For some reason, I was seized by an undeniable urge to touch the figure. I flew toward it, with my hand outstretched.

"What are you doing? You can't touch that," Michael nearly shrieked.

"Why not?" I asked, not bothering to stop.

"Don't you think alarms might go off?"

"If they do, we'll project away. Michael, please, I *have* to touch it."

My fingers grazed the surprisingly grainy surface of the painting. Without warning, I started to experience a flash, as if my fingers had touched someone's skin instead of a wall. Something told me that the flash came directly from Michelangelo's mind. For me.

After it passed and I regained control of myself, I whispered, "I know what the message is, Michael."

"How?"

"By touching this figure. This is the place where Michelangelo received his vision from God."

"Michelangelo imbedded a flash in a painting? And it survived all these centuries? After all the restoration it's been subjected to?"

"I know it sounds incredible. But it's true."

"What's the message?" He still sounded skeptical.

"This is what the end days will look like if an Elect One controlled by the Dark Fallen judges the end. This is what the end days will look like if we don't succeed. If we fail, humankind will not be given room for second chances. There will be no forgiveness, no redemption, except for those who agree to serve the Dark Fallen. They are determined to reign here on earth forever, since they know they will never rule in heaven. To do so, they must control the end. By controlling me."

Together, we stared at the figure. The man's agony was so real, so painful, I could almost feel the hellfire upon me. I'd been so focused on me—finding out who I was, developing my skills, figuring out where I stood with the recently mercurial Michael—that I hadn't stepped back and reflected on the why, the big picture. Michelangelo's message made the stakes very tangible. Very personal.

I looked over at Michael. "Michael, we can't let that happen. We can't let our parents and Ruth and everyone we have ever loved end up like this poor figure. Given how hard our parents have worked for grace, don't they deserve a chance at redemption? Don't we all?"

Michael stared back at me, his eyes brimming with emotion. For humankind and for me. "Yes, Ellie, they do. So do we."

I reached out for his hand, and squeezed it tight. Maybe I wouldn't have to wait until "after" for us to stand together as the soul mates we were meant to be. "Together, we'll protect them."

TWENTY-SEVEN

I awoke with the strongest sensation of peace and happiness. For a decadent minute, I allowed myself to relive the moment in the Sistine Chapel when Michael and I locked eyes and hands. I had felt closer to him than I had in some time. Maybe that had been Rafe's goal, or one of his goals, anyway.

I showered and dressed as quickly as possible. Gathering up my homework, phone, and keys and sticking them in my bag, I rushed out into the hallway. I couldn't wait to see Michael today.

As I descended the stairs, I swore I heard the television. In our house, we had one small television in the kitchen that my parents permitted me to use for the sole purpose of catching the news, like watching some of the earthquake coverage. My parents never, ever watched it in the morning, though.

The second I walked into the kitchen, my mom shut

it off. Not before I saw a newscaster making a breaking announcement before the backdrop of a spewing volcano. My heart sank. Had Ruth's prediction come true?

"What was that, Mom?"

"Nothing, dearest," she answered. Averting my gaze, she returned to buttering my toast.

"Please put the TV back on for a minute, Mom."

Reluctantly, she picked up the remote and flicked the television on. In horror, I listened to the newscaster describe a dormant volcano on an island off the coast of Greenland that had erupted without warning in the night. More startling were the images of its explosion. Lightning streaked across the volcano's top as ruby-red lava flowed down its side, all against the backdrop of an enormous, billowing ash cloud. The scene left me shaken and speechless.

Ruth had been absolutely correct, eerily so. Now that I'd seen firsthand the deadly havoc the fallen angels could wreak, my newly restored confidence faltered. I'd failed with Kael, and this catastrophe was the result. How could I do battle against the fallen who possessed such might?

The path of the volcano's initial destruction was vast but nothing compared to the worldwide destruction that could be inflicted in the coming hours and days. According to the newscaster, famine and disease could result if the ash plume expanded and blanketed the European skies as top scientists calculated it would. Just as Ruth had forecast.

Now I knew why Rafe risked using our powers outside the field last night. It no longer mattered if the fallen knew where we were or what we were doing. The second and third seal had been opened, and maybe others. There was no more reason to hide.

When Michael arrived in his car to pick me up for school, we decided to cut class to find Rafe. We desperately needed to talk to him. Figuring that the field was our best shot at locating him, we raced directly there.

As we hurtled down the narrow Tillinghast back roads toward the field, I thought of Ruth. She would be worried sick by the reports of the volcanic eruption; better than anyone else in the world, other than me and Michael, she understood the true impact of the news. A huge part of me longed to reassure her in person, although I knew a text would have to suffice.

I quickly typed into my cell, "You were right. Please don't worry. We're going to take care of everything."

The words weren't much, but they were all I could offer.

The second I stopped typing, my cell beeped. Poor Ruth must have been staring at her phone, waiting for my message. "I can't stop worrying. So please take care of yourself. And all of us."

I started to write her back, when the car suddenly lurched to a stop and Michael cried out, "He's here."

Thank God, Rafe did not disappoint.

"Did you see the news?" Michael asked the second we were in yelling distance.

"I didn't need the news to tell me that more seals have been broken," Rafe answered more quietly.

"You knew that this was coming last night, didn't you?" I asked.

"Yes. I also knew that we couldn't stop the breaking of those seals. The decision to launch those events had been made days ago."

The import of Rafe's words settled upon me. Kael. The seals.

I shook my head and muttered, "Two more seals opened."

"Yes, Ellspeth. Famine and disease. Kael had control over those two signs," Rafe informed me.

"This is all my fault."

"No, Ellie. You can't possibly be to blame." Michael tried to comfort me.

"Michael, the fallen angel from the other night, Kael. He's the one who released these signs. If I could have stopped him . . ." I couldn't finish.

Rafe grabbed me by the shoulders and stared me in the

eyes. "Ellspeth, listen to me. I told you before. You couldn't possibly have prevented Kael's actions. At the time he made contact with you, you didn't know how to destroy him. The wheels of his destruction were already in motion. Swaying you would've been a bonus prize."

"Surely the others will come soon. If Ruth is right and Kael's volcano triggers two signs, then we still have four more angels to worry about. Wouldn't Kael have told them where to find me?"

"The fallen don't exactly cooperate, except to keep the end-days wheels in motion. Otherwise, it's every fallen for himself, in terms of persuading you, anyway. You see, Ellspeth, the fallen who secures you is the fallen who wields the most power at the end."

"But—"

"No more buts. We have only limited time left to prepare before your battles will commence. Let's not spend it on useless regrets." He gave me a small smile. "Or endless questions."

As Rafe spoke, I watched Michael's fists clench and unclench. He appeared willing to fly off that very minute to fell a battalion of fallen angels. "I'm ready, Rafe. I'll do anything to protect my Ellie. How will we find them?"

"My Ellie." It seemed so long ago that Michael last used those words. Perhaps our evening in the Sistine Chapel really had bridged the strange divide of petty jealousies and football and who knows what else that had formed between us since we returned from Boston.

"You won't need to seek them out, Michael."

"What do you mean?"

"The fallen need Ellspeth to fulfill their objectives, as you know. *They* are looking for you. Undoubtedly, they have sensed the powers you exercised last night outside the field. And I'm sure they sensed Kael's failure to secure Ellspeth. Tracking you and Ellspeth won't prove particularly challenging."

"So?"

"So Michael, they are coming. The fallen will find you and Ellspeth. We just need to be ready."

Twenty-eight

We spent the rest of the day and night practicing aerial maneuvers, mental blocking techniques, and weaponry skills until my limbs begged for relief. For once, I didn't complain. Rafe had intimated that this was one of our last nights of training, and I could not afford to waste a single piece of Rafe's celestial wisdom.

I started to attempt a particularly tricky sword exercise under Michael's tutelage, when I heard Rafe yell, "Come. We must go."

It couldn't be that close to daybreak. Glancing down at my watch, I saw that it was only two o'clock, too early for breaking up. "Why are we leaving? I want to practice that one last—"

"They're waiting, Ellspeth."

"Who, Rafe? Who is waiting?" I was getting pretty tired of the mysteries. I knew Rafe had his reasons for doling out information in an enigmatic, molasses-like fashion, but my entire being told me we neared the end. There was no time for his obscurities.

"Your parents."

"Our parents?" Michael sounded as shocked as I felt. I'd asked a couple days ago if we could tell them, and Rafe had categorically denied me. Why would they be coming to meet us now?

"Yes. I informed Hananel, Daniel, Armaros, and Sariel that we'd meet them tonight. I told you that I would let them know when it was time."

Before I could ask any number of questions, Rafe took to the air. Michael and I followed him as he vacated our protected field for the skies over Tillinghast. Funny how quickly and expertly Rafe had schooled us; we no longer flew in his wake.

I glimpsed the town library and the Daily Grind beneath us, and in the far, far distance, the coast. It had been so long since Michael and I visited Ransom Beach. Would we ever have the luxury of going there again?

The three of us circled over the town green. I assumed we were making some wide turns before heading to some secluded, coastal spot, until I glanced down. A couple dozen people inhabited the green. What were they doing here at this hour? Why would Rafe have allowed us to fly near a crowd? Even worse, why would he schedule a reunion with our parents in such a populated place?

Then I looked again. The town green wasn't occupied by ordinary people at all. From their luminous attractiveness and the faint arcs of light emitting from some backs, I saw that they were angels. My parents and Michael's parents stood at the center of their circle.

As we lowered ourselves to the ground, I asked Rafe, "Who are all those angels? Are they like you?"

"No, Ellspeth, they are the Light Fallen. Unlike the Dark Fallen, they are striving for redemption and His light. Like your parents."

"There's so many of them. I thought my parents and Michael's parents were some of a very few."

"Twenty-five of the original two hundred are striving for grace. All the Light Fallen are standing on the town green."

"Why are they here?"

He gave me that rakish smile I'd been drawn to since the first day we met. "They wanted to meet the Elect One."

Our feet touched down on the soft grass covering the town green. Hesitantly, I walked toward the circle enclosing my waiting parents. Angels parted as I strode through their ranks. I recognized Tamiel from Boston, who smiled at me. Some nodded their heads reverentially, while others reached out to touch me gently, like my skin alone bestowed a blessing. I felt strange, like they thought I was someone I clearly was not.

My parents stood patiently with their arms outstretched. The angels' attention made me feel peculiar. I was supposed to be this strong, impervious Elect One, capable of saving them all. I wasn't sure what to say or how to act.

Until I collapsed into a sobbing heap in my parents' arms. There—despite all my strides in confidence in becoming the Elect One—I became regular Ellie. Daniel and Hannah's awkward teenage daughter.

My mom spoke first. "I'm so sorry that we had to try and make you forget who you truly are—again. After everything that happened in Boston, everyone thought it would slow down the advance of the end days if you forgot. We thought it would protect you . . and everyone else."

"We're so sorry that it didn't work. And that you were left all alone to pretend to be a regular teenage girl, when you probably had so many questions and were so scared," my more-emotional dad sputtered.

"I know," I managed to say through my tears. And I did understand. "Rafe explained everything to me. Thank you for everything. You made so many sacrifices to raise me. I know what you gave up." The thought of their forgone immortality made me cry even harder.

My dad squeezed me tighter, if that was possible. "Ellie,

it was not a sacrifice but a gift and a privilege to raise you. Never thank us."

"It seems so unfair that you and Michael must fight the fallen alone, even if the prophecy dictates it. I wish we could stand alongside you and fight," my mom said, her voice cracking. It was hard listening to the sadness evident in her usually imperturbable voice. "Instead of being a liability."

I understood what my mom meant, even though she hadn't spelled it out. She and my dad were afraid that the fallen would use them as bait.

"Don't worry, Mom. Michael and I can protect you. Rafe has taught us some pretty amazing moves."

Despite all the heaviness in the air, my dad chortled. "My gorgeous, bright, clumsy daughter protecting us? I'd like to see that." I knew he was only kidding.

"You needn't worry about us, Ellie," my mom was quick to add. "The other fallen striving for grace will protect us, to ensure that we don't become pawns in this ugly game."

"They'll watch out for you too, my dearest. They will be limited in what kind of help they can offer—because the prophecy requires that only you and Michael destroy the key fallen, of course—but the Light Fallen can advise and get messages to us. Although, I don't know how much help that'll be." My dad wanted to offer some assistance, no matter how limited.

So that was the reason the Light Fallen had assembled. It was for my parents' protection. I had been wondering, since they could not help us destroy the necessary Dark Fallen. Despite what Rafe claimed, I seriously doubted that they simply wanted to meet the Elect One.

My mom continued: "Don't worry about us, Ellie. You focus on doing your job."

I almost laughed; she sounded like she was giving me one of her famous pre-exam pep talks. The laughter evaporated when I caught some of the expectant expressions on the angels' faces.

I shifted my gaze to the ground. "I hope I can do everything that you all think I can."

My mom lifted up my chin. "We *know* you can, Ellie. You were born to do this."

The word "born" caught my attention. Knowing that I might never have another chance to raise the question that had been burning in my mind for weeks now, I asked, "Who are my parents?"

My parents glanced at each other, each seeking permission to reveal the long-buried secret. My mom, ever the tougher of the two, spoke for them both. "Your mother was a beautiful human woman named Elle."

"Elle?"

My mom smiled at the question. "Yes, we named you

Ellspeth in her honor."

I liked that. "What was she like?"

"We knew her for a very short time. She had long, straight blond hair, just like yours except for the color. She was smart and brave—and very young."

"Why do you say she was brave?"

"All alone, she brought you into the world, knowing exactly who and what you were. And she never faltered."

My eyes welled with tears, thinking of my poor birth mother. Even though I knew the answer—Tamiel had told me as much, in Boston—I needed to ask the question. "Where is she now?"

"She died giving birth to you, Ellie. I am so sorry." I could tell that delivering the news was very difficult for my stoic mom.

"What about my birth father? He's a fallen angel, right?"

"Yes, he is."

Suddenly, a possibility occurred to me. One more palatable than the alternative. "Is my father here? Is he one of the Light Fallen, like you?"

"No, dearest, he isn't," my dad jumped in. "If it's any consolation, I do believe that your father loved your mother."

My mom paused and added, "In his way."

More questions bombarded my already overloaded consciousness. Yet when I studied my parents' faces, they had expressions of such grief, I couldn't ask them. I couldn't waste my precious minutes with them talking about my birth parents. *They* were my real parents. Instead I grabbed them tight.

Out of the corner of my eye, I spotted Michael with his parents. Although they shed no tears—Michael was such a *guy*, after all—I saw that their reunion was bittersweet as well. It was perhaps the last time we were our true Nephilim selves with our parents.

TWENTY-NINE

After our parents and their phalanx of angels dispersed, Michael and I realized that we had one spare hour before the dawn. One hour before we assumed the facade of normal teenagers for one last day. One hour before the end-days battle loomed on every corner. One hour to be alone.

"Ransom Beach," he whispered in my ear as we left the town green.

Clasping his hand tightly in mine, we lifted off without a word. We whipped by the recognizable markers—the vast stretch of the tide, the steep coastal cliffs, the craggy stones bordering the shore. They acted as a pathway to our sacred place. The place where Michael first showed me he could fly. The place where we revealed our true selves to each other—angel and human.

We lowered ourselves down on the cliff overlooking the beach and ocean. The air smelled of brine. There was no whiff of sun-baked sand, the remnants of which we'd detected on our last visit. No mournful cry of seagulls sounded. Winter had already laid claim to this isolated, rough stretch of cove and sea.

Michael and I linked hands. Together, we walked to the very edge of the precipitous cliff face for which Ransom Beach was known. Then we dove. Like we had done forever ago.

Funny how small the cliff seemed after our nights spent in the dizzying vertical world of Rafe's design. We touched down softly on the rocky sand, and then instinctively headed to the protective arms of the cliff's baseline boulders where we'd spent many evenings.

There, we embraced. We just stood there and hugged.

"We've wasted so much time separated from each other. Separated in spirit, I mean," I whispered.

"I know, Ellie. And I'm not sure why."

"Me neither."

Michael's voice became gravelly as he said, "Then let's not waste a single second more."

Slowly, Michael ran his hands up and down my arms, then through my hair. Staring into my eyes, he traced his finger along my chin, cheeks, and lips. Finally, he leaned toward me and brushed his full lips against mine. The gentle motion sent shivers up my spine, and I wanted more.

I kissed him hard. Immediately, his mouth grew eager,

parting my lips ever so slightly and running his tongue along mine. My breath labored as I realized what was coming. We no longer had any reason to hold back.

I touched his tongue with my own. Then I ran my tongue along his teeth, while he did the same. Our blood mingled, and a familiar warmth bathed me. It drew me closer and closer to him, in body and spirit. With my hands lost in his hair and my mouth locked on his, the warmth transformed into a blinding light. The light of a vision.

In my mind's eye, the light softened enough that I could discern the setting. We were walking along a beach. It reminded me of Ransom Beach, except that the sand was soft and white, and waves lapped at the shore rather than crashing as they usually did. Michael and I were holding hands, and bright letters were emblazoned on our chests. Letters from another language.

Nothing like this had ever happened in real life. It looked more like my dreams. Was it some flash of the future?

Without warning, the light darkened, and the scene changed. I saw jarring images from Michael's mind, more like the disjointed flashes I got from touching people. I watched as Michael huddled with his football coach after the recent victory. I couldn't see Coach Samuel's face, but I heard his voice lavishing praise on Michael and describing him as a gifted hero to everyone on the team and in the community. He described the heights to which Michael could soar, on the football field and beyond. Michael lapped up the tributes like a puppy. And like a puppy, Michael could think of little else but that attention.

After the flash of Michael and his coach faded, I felt something unusual, almost like images were being extracted from my mind. Scenes started to pour out—snippets of my first meeting with Rafe in the Tillinghast gymnasium, a picture of Rafe and me laughing while we solicited donations from the townspeople for the benefit, the moment when Rafe first revealed his angelic nature to me, and the night when Rafe appeared at my bedroom window and flew away with me.

Abruptly, the flash stopped, and Michael and I pulled apart from each other. How had those images been transported to Michael? I hadn't been thinking about them when Michael and I shared blood. Had someone else removed them intentionally? Had Michael learned to do that from Rafe? Had he figured out how to do that on his own?

Michael and I stared into each other's eyes. Anger passed across his face. Hurriedly, I started to offer excuses, explanations for the flashes he'd obviously seen. He opened his mouth, and suddenly I felt something on my back.

The first blow.

THIRTY

Michael and I had forgotten Rafe's very first rule: never, ever let your guard down.

I spun around to face the attacker. A fallen angel—golden curls framing his chiseled features and wearing an improbably gorgeous shearling jacket to ward off the cold night air—stood before me. He didn't move or speak, and it dawned on me that his beauty alone would probably influence most humans. Without taking my eyes off him, I stepped back slowly to see if Michael could help.

Michael was busy. Another fallen—one with short brown hair atop an angular, attractive face—hovered behind him. It was every man for himself.

Fear started to take hold. I'd grown in self-assurance since we started training, but even so, I wasn't sure I could do this on my own. Even Rafe had his doubts about my fighting abilities; that was why he constantly admonished Michael to stay by my side. That wasn't an option right now. Maybe that was why these particular fallen chose the divide-and-conquer approach.

I knew that I couldn't allow fear to paralyze me. All would be lost. Purposefully, I evoked Rafe's words about Him choosing me—almost like a mantra—and I took to the skies.

Rafe had advised me to conduct our battle in the heavens, so I soared directly upward. As I passed through the thick stratus cloud layer into the puffier cumulus layer, I did not turn back to see if the fallen pursued me. I knew he had.

In my peripheral vision, I saw that Michael followed Rafe's advice too. Or perhaps he was simply heading in the direction he knew that I'd have to go. I watched as Michael's natural speed allowed him to climb higher and higher, his pursuer in close chase. Michael swooped and turned and pivoted through the sky with such ability that the fallen could not keep pace. I imitated Michael's patterns as best I could, and even though I couldn't match Michael's speed or his aerial maneuvers, the fallen angel tracking me lagged behind as well.

I knew that evasion could only work for so long. As did Michael. We both needed to get closer to the supernatural creatures. We needed to draw their blood. I racked my brain for an applicable strategy from Rafe's tutorials, without success.

I didn't even have a weapon. Rafe's impressive lineup of armaments certainly wasn't floating around in the sky over Ransom Beach.

Then I remembered what I had in my pocket. A game plan came to me. It would require that I put all my practice at playacting to good use. Maybe that was what Rafe meant as one of my human advantages?

Cloud by cloud, I slowed my pace, almost imperceptibly at first. I wanted the fallen to think I was still flying flat out. Feigning fatigue, I permitted the blond angel to catch up with me. I then allowed him to grasp my wrist with his cold, ethereal hand. Locked together, we hovered in the air.

Pretending to wrench my wrist free, I actually let him come within inches of my face. I believed that, in such close proximity, the creature would be tempted to use his persuasive powers. He craved my support, after all. The fallen did not disappoint.

"Ellspeth, I am Barakel. I have waited so long for you to join me. Together, we can stop the downward spiral of financial destitution that has gripped this world and that will continue to pull this world into abject poverty if we don't halt it. Together, we can create a world in which money will no longer matter. Together, we can fashion an earth where there will be no more physical wants, no more physical needs, only the luxury to pursue your dreams."

This time, I would not be lured in by false promises, as I'd almost been with Kael.

His long, elegant fingers caressed the palm of my hand, and I noticed that his own wrist was encased in a heavy, gold Cartier watch. Clearly, Barakel already had the financial luxury to pursue his dreams. After all, he was Barakel, the Dark Fallen in charge of the fourth seal of economic depression. He had no intention of sparing humankind a single second of destitution; instead, he meant to inflict it.

His voice then took on that lulling, singsong quality I'd heard from Ezekiel and Kael. "Come with me, Ellspeth. Imagine the world that we can create together."

Barakel pressed his fingers deeper into my palm. Through his touch, he transmitted a most intoxicating vision. I saw the ivy-covered university town of my dreams—not unlike Cambridge—in which students of all ages, all glowing with physical health and well-being, exchanged ideas at their leisure. Then I saw that university setting being replicated in cities and towns across the globe, over and over again.

I did not want to find Barakel's suggestions attractive. Yet I knew that I needed to allow myself a moment of surrender in order to be believable. So I allowed myself to think that perhaps I *would* like to stand at Barakel's side. Perhaps I would like to rule over a world in which all physical needs and wants were satisfied, a world in which exalted goals were freely pursued. As Barakel paused to gauge my reaction, he stopped his hypnotic chatter.

The quiet allowed my mind to clear for a split second. I steeled myself against the potency of Barakel's voice and the power of his images, and fashioned a mental barricade around my thoughts. Precisely as Rafe had taught me. I answered him. "You want me to join you?"

"Yes, Ellspeth. You belong with me . . ." He stretched out the fingers of his other hand. "Come."

I floated toward him ever so slowly, almost in a trance-like state. As I drew nearer, I lengthened my arm across the remaining distance, as if reaching for Barakel. Finger by finger I stretched in his direction. All except my thumb, which held the keys from my pocket pressed against my palm. My secret weapon.

Patiently, Barakel awaited me. I had no confidence that I could pull this off, but I had no alternative. Brute strength would never work for me, as Rafe himself admitted.

Self-doubt caused my hand to quiver. I got scared that Barakel would notice, and that would reveal my ruse. I didn't think the hands of those truly in his sway would shake. I bet that they simply listened and followed his commands.

Mustering up my courage, I steadied my hand and feigned total submission. "Barakel, I am ready."

As soon as I brushed my fingers along his arm, ready to use my key, I heard a scream.

THIRTY-ONE

I panicked, thinking that it came from Michael. Yet as I listened more closely, I realized that it had an unnatural quality that wasn't quite human. I prayed that the scream came from the other fallen. And that Michael was the cause.

I pretended that I hadn't heard it. I returned to my game of clasping Barakel's hand, and playacting capitulation. But my split-second hesitation—my straining to hear if the voice belonged to Michael—had given me away.

"How dare you!" Barakel seethed.

He lunged for me. The sudden assault left me totally unprepared. Rafe had assured me that the fallen wouldn't attack, that they'd try to woo me instead, and I'd banked on that. I dove away to avoid him, but the maneuver threw me off balance. I started to tumble downward, spinning out of control, and plunging headlong toward the ground.

Familiar landmarks of Ransom Beach—the enormous boulders, the steep cliff from which Michael dove—got closer and closer, and I became more and more terrified. I desperately tried to remember how Rafe had helped me right myself that night I nearly crashed headfirst into the ground. Mimicking his motions as best I could, I managed to sweep my feet underneath me and turn myself right side up mere seconds before I hit, although not before the key plunged into the sea, and my plan along with it.

What was I going to do? I desperately wanted to retreat— to hear the crunch of the rough sand of Ransom Beach under my feet and gather my thoughts—but I couldn't let another fallen angel escape. I thought about the hunger and disease that loomed because I didn't kill Kael. And I had a pretty good idea about the economic depression of epic proportions that would happen if Barakel got away.

I steeled myself for a battle with no game plan and no certainty of victory. Racing through the heavens, I searched for Barakel. His fair hair glinted in the low light of the quarter moon and led me to him. I flew close enough to see the whiteness of his skin and the steely gaze of his hazel eyes. He was furious about my deception, and Rafe had forewarned us about angry angels.

Barakel hurled himself at me. He was strong, and it took all my might to stand my ground against him. Even though I couldn't imagine how he planned to sway me through force, I guessed he had some backup plan to secure my allegiance. I prayed that a weapon would present itself on Barakel's person, as well as an opportunity to draw blood, before he succeeded.

Suddenly, a fearsome cry sounded in the sky. It was very different from the bloodcurdling shriek of moments before. It was triumphant. And warlike.

It was Michael.

"Stay back, Ellie," he called to me.

Michael swooped in. He plucked Barakel out of the sky with a furious abandon. The two locked onto each other so tightly that I couldn't see where one began and the other ended.

I wanted to help, but was ever conscious of my limitations, of the liability I would be to Michael if I became too involved in their fight. Despite Michael's admonitions to keep my distance, I stayed close.

In horror, I watched as Barakel extricated himself from Michael's grasp and pitched him across the sky. Barakel shot me a victorious look, and started off in my direction. I would not be intimidated. The second Barakel reached me, I clutched at his arm, desperate to hold him until Michael could reach us. Hooking my fingers around Barakel's heavy gold Cartier watch, I held on for dear life.

Michael reached my side. With a deft stroke, he flicked out the knife from his switchblade and ran it along Barakel's exposed arm, the one I'd locked onto. Blood beaded on Barakel's perfectly formed wrist. Michael reached out and caught some droplets before they fell away. Then, in one expert motion, Michael licked the blood from his finger and cut Barakel's throat.

The fallen soundlessly plummeted to the earth.

THIRTY-TWO

I froze as I watched Barakel plummet onto the jagged boulders that overlooked Ransom Beach. Unable to tear my eyes from the sight of the fallen's limp body splayed upon the enormous rocks, I hovered in the sky. Only when Michael slipped his hand in mine did I move.

Gently he guided me back to our cove on Ransom Beach. Once I felt the ground solidly beneath my feet, I started shaking uncontrollably. Out of relief or fear, I wasn't certain. The carefully controlled, strong Ellie—the one I fashioned every day since returning from Boston—had crumbled. And I was furious with myself.

"How am I supposed to fulfill the prophecy, Michael? I don't think I can do it. You saw that I can't do it."

"You can, Ellie. And you will."

"You had to kill Barakel for me. I should have been able to do that myself."

"Don't be too hard on yourself, Ellie. You did stand your

ground against Barakel. I bet if I hadn't been there, you'd have been able to beat him. Anyway, didn't Ezekiel say that I needed to be a 'knight to my lady?'"

The words brought me back. I simply couldn't let myself dissolve like this. "You definitely were my knight today, Michael. And so much more. Thank you."

"Ellie, never thank me for the privilege of helping you." He smiled. "Anyway, next time, I bet you won't even need my assistance. Even though I'll be there if you do."

I took a deep breath at the thought of the three remaining fallen. I'd have to remain strong so I could better handle this again and again. "Next time."

Michael held me in his arms. In our sheltered cove, we hung on to each other and waited. Even though neither of us said it, I think we both expected some confirmation that we had stopped two signs by killing two more fallen.

"Nothing's changed," I finally said. I couldn't stand the silence—and the unspoken disappointment—a second longer.

"I know," Michael answered. He knew exactly what I meant. "The wind, the surf. It's all exactly the same as . . ."

He trailed off, and didn't finish his sentence. So I did it for him. "Before. Before you killed the two fallen."

"Yeah. I guess I thought that if we killed two of the fallen angels responsible for the signs, we'd get some sort of signal that we'd put a dent in the end days."

"Me too. If we destroyed two of the key fallen, that is."

"What do you mean?" He sounded confused.

"Maybe the Dark Fallen capable of triggering the signs have other fallen that help them? I'm guessing that the one you killed first was a helper for Barakel—the one who came for me."

"It seems like we won't know if we're successful until the very end," Michael said sadly.

"Yes." I hated to agree, although it now seemed undeniably true.

There were no words of consolation or encouragement I could offer. Nothing more than the comfort of my embrace. We stood quietly for a moment, until the wind picked up. Michael wrapped his arms around me tighter. The heat of his breath on my hair warmed me and made me hopeful that things could be right between us.

Regardless of our close brush with death, the respite from the flashes of me with Rafe was short-lived.

"Ellie, what's going on with you and Rafe? Those flashes, well, they were really upsetting." Michael's voice cracked.

My heart broke a tiny bit to hear the sadness in his voice. It was so much worse than his anger. "Michael, I know how the flashes must have looked . . ."

"You don't know how they looked. And you can't know how they felt."

I clung to him. "Please Michael, believe me. Nothing

happened between me and Rafe."

Michael stared into my eyes, searching for the truth. He must have found something genuine in them—something to believe in—because he touched his lips to mine. We started gently kissing, and I felt our connection strengthen. I thought we could get over whatever pain those flashes had caused him.

But then another figure landed on Ransom Beach.

Rafe.

THIRTY-THREE

Without thinking, without even hesitating, I raced across the rocky sand dunes to meet Rafe. I wanted to tell him what happened and get a million questions answered — especially whether Barakel and the other fallen that Michael had killed represented one or two of the remaining signs.

Before I could even get a word out, Michael yelled out behind me, "Can't wait a single second?"

I spun around. "What are you talking about, Michael?"

"The flashes, Ellie. Remember?" he said, pointing to Rafe. "Plus, I've watched how he looks at you."

How Rafe looks at me? Michael didn't know what he was talking about. Rafe didn't care for me, other than in his official angelic capacity. I could understand Michael's anger at the frisson of attraction that passed between me and Rafe in those flashes he experienced, even though nothing had happened. I wished Michael could confidently draw on the love we felt for each other, rather than automatically thinking the worst of me. Yet, I could hardly be disappointed in him for not doing so; I'd had my own doubts about Michael over the past few days too.

Still, I wanted us to keep the connection we'd reforged. I didn't want to divide us again by arguing with his logic. So I started to explain.

"Michael, please don't jump to conclusions. Let me—" I begged.

He cut me off. "Ellie, please don't patronize me with some weak explanations. Pictures speak louder than words."

Rafe jumped in. "Michael, nothing inappropriate happened between Ellspeth and myself."

Inflicting his wrath on Rafe, Michael shouted, "I know that. I'm not talking about what did happen. I'm talking about what *you* wanted to happen, Rafe. Anyway, why should I believe anything you say? How do I know that you're not one of the six fallen, and you're not using all this training as a way to have us get rid of the others for you? So you can stand alone with your precious Ellspeth—who you've already swayed—at the end?"

"Michael, please!" I was aghast at the accusations he wielded against me and Rafe together, and against Rafe alone.

"Think about it, Ellie. How do we know that Rafe is

who he says he is? You should be careful not to trust him as easily as you do."

"Michael, I know he's not a fallen. I know he is pure angel."

Michael put his hands on his hips. "Just because he told you so?"

I was afraid to tell him, but it was the only way to convince Michael. "No. Because I saw it in his blood."

Michael's face turned ashen. "You drank his blood?"

"I had to, Michael. It was the only way I could be certain that we could trust him."

Michael's body started to transform for flight. His shoulder blades expanded and his arms lengthened. I knew it would be painful for him to hear about the blood, but after what we'd been through—after all we still faced—would he actually leave me? Was it for tonight, or forever?

"Good-bye, Rafe. I don't think your training is necessary anymore. I handled myself pretty well out there tonight against two of the fallen. And, Ellie, I don't think I can be around you right now."

"Michael, don't leave!" I beseeched him. I couldn't believe that he'd actually take off.

Michael looked over at me. His eyes looked so mournful yet so fixed in their judgment.

"Ellie, I cannot sit around and watch Rafe gaze at you

through one more so-called session, knowing what I now know. Day is about to break. I think I'll spend tomorrow night practicing on the football field instead."

"No, Michael."

"Why not, Ellie? That's where my skills are appreciated."

"Michael, I am so grateful for your skills and for you. You saved my life. You *are* my life."

"Is that why you left my arms for Rafe the minute he arrived? Is that why you willingly drank his blood? When you know all too well how the blood can make you feel? If I was truly your life, I don't think you would have done any of those things."

I started to object, when Rafe stilled me. Even though I knew Rafe was right—that my entreaties would fall on deaf ears—it killed me to let Michael go.

But I had to.

THIRTY-FOUR

I wanted to curl into the comfort of Rafe's powerful chest and cry. I wanted to cry for the loss of the teenager Ellie, who innocently loved travel and books and movies. For the forced emergence of her replacement, the Nephilim Ellspeth, who needed to be strong and invincible to fulfill the prophecy. Most of all, for the casualty caused by that transformation: the relationship between me and Michael.

But I didn't want to give credence to Michael's accusations by finding solace in Rafe's arms. Instead, I tried to assume the role of the indomitable Nephilim.

I mustered up some bravado, put my hands on my hips, and said to Rafe, "What will I do now? I thought that the prophecy required both me and Michael. And you can see that I need him. He's the one who killed the two fallen tonight. Michael's the one who stopped at least one sign. Not me."

Michael's flight—literal and figurative—hadn't fazed

Rafe. He seemed impervious to the changeability of humankind, one of the few qualities about him that was very different when he was an angel.

He answered me calmly, "Michael did help to stop the fourth sign. Barakel could've triggered a worldwide economic crisis. Ellspeth, please don't worry. Michael will play his most important role when the time comes."

"How can you be so sure?"

"God foretold it through His word. And He's very rarely wrong."

"What about free will? Didn't the fallen exercise their free will against His wishes?"

"God does allow for free will. Yet, I feel like I've gotten to know you and Michael well enough that I believe your will is in accord with His word."

What else had He deigned to tell Rafe? I had a sneaking suspicion that Rafe was holding back. "Did He make any predictions as to whether Michael would love me after all this is over? Assuming I do my job, that is. Did He foretell that?"

"His word only divulges that which is necessary," Rafe said with a small smile that I'm sure he thought was consoling.

I wasn't comforted. I wanted to scream. I hated it when Rafe slipped into angel speak, and, anyway, all his mysterious predictions and evasive answers were making me mad. And wary.

What if Michael was right? What if all this training and reassurance and affection were ruses on Rafe's part? What if he was only acting this way to make me align with him, so that I would stand by *his* side when he undid the seventh seal? What if Rafe was able to use his blood to trick me? Maybe it was time for a challenge.

I squared my shoulders and stared at him straight on. "If you know so much, why don't you tell me about this mysterious role that Michael will play?"

"I don't know, Ellspeth. He hasn't shared that with me."

"He must have uncovered his precious timeline to you, as an angel of His presence," I taunted him. "You must know when the remaining fallen will come for me, for example."

At the mention of the angels of His presence, Rafe's face clouded over with sorrow. "No, Ellspeth. He only revealed to me what I've already told you. But I think that you'll know the Dark Fallen when you encounter them. Just like you did with the others you've come across."

"Oh yeah, I did such a great job identifying Ezekiel. I had no idea who he was until it was too late. Same with Kael. Anyway, I don't believe you, Rafe, when you say that you've already told me everything that He told you. I may only be half an angel—not a full breed like you—but even I can tell when you're keeping secrets. If you know anything else—especially signs that will help me recognize the Dark Fallen—now is the time to tell me."

He hesitated. And Rafe never hesitated. "Maybe it's time that I share something else with you."

"Maybe it is," I said angrily. Finally, after all these games and obfuscations, we were getting to the truth.

"Only you can destroy the fallen responsible for the seventh seal. Not Michael. He won't be capable of doing so."

Rafe's disclosure surprised me. I thought he'd give me some basic tips on spotting a Dark Fallen in a crowd. Not something of this magnitude.

"Why? Why wouldn't Michael be able to kill the last one?" As I spoke the words aloud, a horrible possibility occurred to me. Maybe Michael wouldn't be able to slay the final fallen, because he would be slain himself.

"Will he be—" I couldn't even finish my question.

Rafe understood. "No, Michael's death won't be the reason that you must deliver the ultimate blow. I don't know why he cannot help you. I haven't been told."

I looked into his mournful, angelic eyes, and saw he spoke the truth. It happened to be a hard truth, one I did not want to hear. But then I saw a flicker of something else in Rafe's eyes. Something I nearly missed. Something that he was trying very hard to hide.

"That's it? You're sure there's nothing else you're holding back from me?"

He stared down at the ground.

"Tell me, Rafe." I took my hands off my hips and reached out for his. "Please, there's no time left for secrets. Not if you want me to succeed."

A maelstrom of emotions passed across his ethereal face. I could see that this last secret was at the eye of the storm—as was the decision whether or not to share it with me.

He tightened his fingers around mine, and leaned toward me. His lips brushed across my cheek, and I could feel his hair on my forehead. We'd never been so close, not even when I drank his blood. His nearness momentarily drove out thoughts of all else, even the pain of Michael's abandonment.

Rafe began to whisper. At first, I almost couldn't hear the words, because I could think only of the sensation. His soft breath on my ear was so deliciously warm and soothing. "The only secret I've kept is one I don't even want Him to know. Because it's forbidden."

"You can tell me, Rafe. You can tell me anything."

He paused, and then pressed his lips against my ear. "Do you remember the story I told you about the beginning?"

"Yes, I do." I almost didn't care what he said; I wanted

him to keep whispering forever.

"Do you recall that I told you that the angels arrived on earth with the mission to teach and protect? And that changed once they met humankind. Something caused them to fall."

"Yes, of course," I said, even though I was mostly focused on what it would feel like if Rafe's lips traveled down from my ear to my neck.

"I told you that I initially believed that the fallen fell from pride. Pride in their godlike ability to teach and create."

"Yes?"

"I've since learned that it wasn't only pride that caused the fallen to fall."

"What was it, Rafe?" I answered him, half listening.

"It was also love."

I stopped relishing the sensation of his breath in my ear and his lips on my skin, and I looked up. Had he really just said that? Did he mean what I thought he meant?

We stared at each other for a long, silent moment. I should've been surprised by Rafe's words and what they meant. Somewhere, deep within myself, I had suspected them, even feared them. From the very first moment he had told me the story of the fallen and why they fell for humans, I knew he was telling me the story of himself.

"Love," I finally said. "The fallen fell from grace because

they fell in love with humans."

Then Rafe placed his forehead on mine, and we stood close, breathing deeply. Despite my subconscious suspicions, I still couldn't believe that Rafe had actually uttered those words. Even though, if I were truthful with myself, I loved hearing them.

"I love you, Ellspeth. Even though I can never, ever have you."

Rafe's lips moved slowly from my ear to my cheek. He breathed me in—my scent, my very being. I'd never been so close to him, and he smelled so intoxicating, so otherworldly. It was less like a scent and more like a memory. It conjured within me homesickness for a place I'd never been.

I wondered what it would be like to kiss him.

I felt myself weaken, my knees buckle. He wrapped his arm around my back, bolstering me, and I thought I heard the beating of his heart. Yet it sounded unlike the steady beat I'd often heard in Michael's chest. More like the slow, rhythmic flapping of wings.

Was this my real destiny? Michael had become so mercurial, and our relationship had become so difficult lately. Had the past few weeks simply been a long, painful goodbye to Michael? Was I meant to be with Rafe?

Rafe brushed his lips back and forth on my cheek.

Slowly, too slowly, he moved his mouth onto mine. His felt so soft and full and enveloping. Our lips met.

The moment we kissed, a strange lurching sensation passed over me. Two powerful flashes overtook me, almost simultaneously. In one, I stood on Ransom Beach with Michael hand in hand, watching the most vivid, exquisite sunset I've ever seen. Tranquility and joy washed over me. In the other, I stood on that same beach with Michael, although we were not holding hands, and Rafe paced behind us. A hollow feeling inhabited my core, and a dark hailstorm brewed in the darkening sky above the sea.

From wherever—or whoever—the images came, I understood the message. As if he knew what I'd seen, Rafe immediately withdrew.

"I must go, Ellspeth. My presence here is now doing more harm than good. You must repair your relationship with Michael. And together, you must fulfill the prophecy."

He was right. From the moment Rafe's lips touched mine, I knew it was wrong. No matter how furious I was with Michael, that anger was a blip. He and I belonged together.

Still, I didn't want to say good-bye. I closed my eyes, and said, "No, Rafe."

"Ellspeth, more than anything on earth or heaven, I want to stay with you. But you and Michael—it has been foretold since the beginning."

"What about free will, Rafe? What if I want you to stay?" Despite what I'd seen and what I felt, a part of me still wanted Rafe by my side.

His dark eyes bored into mine. "Ellspeth, God granted you free will, as he did to the rest of his creations. Yet I *know* you. I know that you would only exercise that free will to do what is right and good. And you know that means staying with Michael and fulfilling your destiny."

"You are right, Rafe. I know you are," I whispered with a sigh.

I opened my eyes to take one last look into his. But he was gone.

Yet in the sound of the wind whipping across Ransom Beach, I swore I heard Rafe's voice. "I'll be watching you, Ellspeth."

THIRTY-FIVE

I was alone.

Never mind that my mom and dad waited for me anxiously on the stoop of our little Victorian house when I landed after my solitary flight home from Ransom Beach. Never mind that the cell phone on my desk showed that Ruth had left countless texts and voice mails agonizing about the volcano and the fulfillment of her predictions. Never mind that Rafe was out there—somewhere—watching me.

I needed Michael. Not my parents, not Ruth, not even Rafe. Without Michael, my world felt empty. The vision showed me that we belonged together, no matter how we'd grown apart and no matter the distraction of Rafe. The vision showed me the emptiness of a life when Michael and I didn't stand hand in hand. He was my destiny, he was my soul mate. The only one who fully understood and loved the entire Ellie—human and divine.

No matter. It seemed like I'd have to stare evil in the face and defeat it by myself. Unlike the last time I felt utterly isolated from the rest of humanity—in the Tillinghast train station on my way to Boston—I now knew who I was and what I had to do in excruciating detail. That knowledge made my solitude all the more terrifying.

I wanted to crawl under my warm, cozy quilt. Even if it was only for a few minutes. But, after a round of relieved hugs that followed my tale of escape from two fallen angels, my parents explained that it was not to be.

"I'm so sorry, my dearest," my dad muttered into the mess of my hair. "I know this is hard. The other fallen striving for grace—the ones you and Raphael have taken to calling the Light Fallen—believe that you are best hidden by going about your normal day."

I guessed that the others also believed that—to the extent that the remaining fallen hadn't yet tracked me down—hiding in plain teenage sight seemed to be the best vantage point from which I could strike. Still, I couldn't say that to my dad. He was already upset enough.

My mom needed to be certain that I'd gotten the message that I would go to school. She added, "The others also think that they can best guard me and your dad by keeping us separate from you, Ellie."

Apparently, proximity to me would expose my parents

to unnecessary danger and prove a liability for me if the fallen used my mom and dad as weapons against me. I didn't say that either. It would only make them more upset. I simply nodded my acquiescence and headed upstairs to take a shower, while they stood by helplessly.

I'd have to go to school like any other day. It seemed surreal and pointless that I'd have to go through the motions at Tillinghast High. Innocent, teenage Ellie was so far gone that I had no confidence I could summon her up convincingly even for one more day. There was no sense protesting. If one more day of playacting offered my parents fortification from the fate of *The Last Judgment* figure I'd seen—the terrified man ensnared by demons—I would do it. I would do anything to shelter them from the coming storm.

I called upon my courage. I reminded myself that I was the Elect One, that He—whoever, whatever He was— believed in me. Even if I didn't always believe in myself.

After I showered in the hottest water I could tolerate, trying to scrub off the lingering scent of Barakel, I went into my bedroom and pulled on some jeans, a gray T-shirt and sweater, and my favorite boots. It was my most practical outfit, complete with layers for any situation or weather I might face. With care, I packed my black bag, trying to anticipate everything I might need for battle or survival. Then I picked up a Swiss Army knife from the drawer, where I'd tossed a bunch of stuff from our summer trip, and placed it in my bag.

Trying my best at a brave showing, I marched over to my bedroom door to say farewell to my old life. Without an audience, my self-assurance faltered a bit when I put my hand on the doorknob. Before I ventured out into the unknown, I needed one last moment looking at my child-hood bedroom, the place where I'd dreamed about college and boys and future careers. I needed to say good-bye to the teenage Ellie and all she might have been.

I memorized the crumple of my worn-in, flannel bed-sheets and the stripes of weak sunlight filtering through my blinds onto the floor in front of my window. I ran my finger along the window seat where I'd spent so many hours read-ing. I touched the spines of my beloved childhood books, *The Lion, the Witch and the Wardrobe* chief among them.

I was awash in the memories and the loss, until I heard the beep of my cell phone. I fished it out of my bag, and saw a string of texts from Ruth. The most recent was from 5:30 A.M. I wondered if she'd been up all night worrying about me, about everyone.

I clicked the text open. It said, "What's going on? Please contact me. I'm worried sick."

How could I begin to answer her question? So much was going on, where could I even begin? With the confirmation that two more signs had been unsealed, with the destruction of two fallen angels, with a major rift in my relationship with Michael, or with Rafe's confession and departure? Though I toyed with the idea of sharing everything with Ruth, I knew that I couldn't tell her any of these things. All I could do was appease her.

I wrote a simple note. "All's well. I'll see you at school."

My phone beeped back immediately. "What? What does that mean?"

"Trust me," I typed.

With a heavy heart, I left my bedroom and trudged down the stairs. My mom and dad stood at the bottom, waiting to walk me to the family car. My car now. Our hands linked together, and without speaking a word, we walked through the foyer and out the front door.

"We'll be waiting for you, dearest. After," my dad said, as he squeezed me tighter than any normal human should be able to squeeze.

My mom joined in the hug. Then she reached around her neck and unfastened the locket she always wore, the one that held the key to the safe containing proof of my parents' unnaturally long existence. She strung it around my neck, and said, "After."

I couldn't look at either of them. The timbre of their voices told me that they were restraining tears. I couldn't allow myself to weaken.

After I unlocked the front door, I settled into the driver's seat. I suddenly felt guilty for not being brave enough to meet their eyes in farewell. Even though I knew I shouldn't, I craned my neck for one last glimpse of them. As I did, I spotted a new landscaper working on Piper's yard. I didn't know why he caught my attention amid the emotional turmoil. I realized that I recognized him from the town green the night before. He was one of the Light Fallen, here to guard my parents. It gave me comfort that they would be safe.

Off I went. To protect humankind.

Thirty-six

Thank God for Ruth.

She was waiting for me at my locker the minute I walked into school. I knew she was desperate to talk. She'd left me countless texts and voice mails with questions about the news coverage of the volcano off the Greenland coast. Travel had been completely suspended indefinitely and the networks were already reporting the scarcity of produce in European markets and the fear of the rapid spread of a deadly lung disease called silicosis from inhaling the ash. It was all happening precisely as Ruth predicted. And she was understandably freaking out.

"Do you know how worried I've been? First, the news reports the volcano *exactly* as I predicted. As I'm bombarded with those broadcasts, I start to read accounts about the onset of famine and disease. It's all *exactly* as I forecast. Then, you and Michael disappear. Poof. You're not at school, and you don't answer your phone other than a single, cryptic text. I thought the worst: that you and Michael had died trying the stop the volcano."

Ruth paused only to take a breath. It gave her enough time to notice my solemn face. She packed away the rest of her questions and the remainder of her commentary like so much luggage. Instead of voicing her concerns, she grabbed me and hugged me.

Loyal friend that she was, Ruth asked, "What can I do?"

"Walk with me to English?" I pleaded with her.

I knew that Michael was somewhere in this building, roaming the hallways without me, ruminating on some imagined relationship between me and Rafe. I couldn't stand the thought of running into him all by myself. What would I say? Where did we stand with each other? I knew where I wanted to stand with him, but what about him? Funny, how I thought of myself as battle ready to destroy fallen angels, yet couldn't bear the notion of encountering Michael in the hallways of Tillinghast High School.

"That I can handle," she said amiably and painted on a smile, despite the angst I knew she felt.

Ruth linked her arm in mine, and together we made our way down the crowded hallway. We got some stares, even more than the normal glares that I still received daily. I didn't care; this could be the last time that *any* of us walked these halls. The knowledge left me unmoored—especially without Michael—and I needed Ruth to be my anchor to the real world. For a few minutes, anyway, before I dropped off into the abyss of the apocalypse.

Ruth could suppress her questions only for so long. She knew what was at stake. She whispered, "So I was right?"

"About the volcano triggering a couple of signs?" I asked.

"Yes," she whispered back.

"You were right." Even though I wanted to tell her more, I hesitated. I needed to weigh very carefully how much to tell the already frightened Ruth. "We don't need to whisper anymore."

Ruth looked at me with alarm. "Why not? We don't want to alert you-know-who to your powers."

"Pretending won't mask my knowledge. They'll come for me when they're ready. In fact, a couple of them have already tried," I admitted.

"What do you mean?" Ruth's alarm rapidly transformed into terror.

"I learned that the seven signs are activated by specific fallen angels. Before the fallen set a sign off, they will each approach me. They will try to lure me in. It's my job to destroy them before they can do so. That's what the prophecy says anyway."

"How did you learn this stuff? I didn't read anything like this in the Books of Enoch or Jubilees or Revelation."

"It's a long story." I knew better than to get into the whole narrative about Rafe. And Ruth knew better than to push me.

"You said that a couple of the fallen found you. If they know where you are, why don't they all come for you right now?"

"It's complicated. It isn't the easiest task in the world to track me, even when I'm utilizing my powers, although that does seem to help them. It's kind of like chasing a shadow. And the fallen don't exactly work together, even though they have a common goal. They each want me for themselves."

She paused. "How did you get away from the ones that found you, Ellie?"

"How do you think?"

Ruth got quiet as she put the puzzle pieces together. "Isn't Michael supposed to help you?"

"He helped me with the fallen who already attacked. We'll see if he comes to my aid with the ones who will follow. Things aren't exactly great between us right now."

Our conversation delayed us. Ruth and I were the last to arrive to English, and Miss Taunton herself greeted us at the door. Her welcome didn't consist of a warm salutation or a grin. Instead, we got an outstretched palm and a brusque demand. Ruth hastily unzipped her bag, and handed something to her.

"What about your paper, Miss Faneuil?"

Paper? What on earth was she talking about? I'd been kind of preoccupied lately with fending off attacks by fallen angels and trying to stop the apocalypse. This whole high school student ruse was ridiculous and enraging. Confusion and irritation must have been written all over my face.

"Don't tell me you've forgotten your paper on Charlotte Brontë?" Miss Taunton asked with unmistakable glee in her voice. For whatever reason, she didn't like me.

The classroom got quiet, and I swear I heard some of the other kids snicker. Miss Taunton didn't lower her hand. In fact, she reached out and touched mine again.

"I am waiting for your paper, Miss Faneuil."

Her fingers vibrated under my touch. If Miss Taunton spoke another word, I couldn't hear it. If my classmates continued their derision, I was deaf to their laughter. A flash of overwhelming intensity washed over me. All I could see and hear were the images from Miss Taunton's mind.

"Don't go, George. I'm begging you," her voice pleaded pathetically. From the timbre of her voice, I could tell she was young, maybe college age.

I watched as her youthful, manicured fingers clawed at the shirt of a bookish young man. He had unremarkable

light brown hair and sloping shoulders, and surpris-
ingly soulful brown eyes. Even though he looked sad, he
seemed determined.

"Eleanor, I cannot live with your jealousies and nega-
tivity. I am going to take this opportunity to study with
Professor Liebsher in Germany. We need to move on.
This is the best way."

"Please, George, I will change. I know I can."

George peeled her fingers off the lapel of his shirt, and
said, "Good bye, Eleanor. I wish you well."

A series of images followed. I could see that after this
George person left, Eleanor Taunton had cut off the hopeful, youthful part of herself. Over the long, lonely years that
followed, her resentment grew, almost like an addiction.
She fed that addiction with her loathing of the freshness
and promise of her young students. Like me, apparently.

When I opened my eyes, I felt that old, Good Samaritan
sensation—the one I thought I'd lost—descend upon me.
Maybe I could help Miss Taunton seek redemption before
it was too late. Before the end. Anyway, what did I have to
lose?

I drew very close to her. Uncomfortably close. And then,
so that the other kids couldn't hear what I was about to say,
I whispered to her.

"Eleanor." It felt very natural to use her first name, after witnessing her at her most vulnerable moment. "I know you have suffered, and I understand your pain. But clinging to the past and holding on to your animosity won't give you the peace you seek. Or the life you desperately want."

Her eyes widened in surprise and then filled with tears of vulnerability. Out of long habit, Miss Taunton—Eleanor—took refuge in her bitterness. Very quietly, she said, "I cannot imagine what you are talking about, Miss Faneuil. If you believe that this little game will buy you an extension for your paper, you are sorely mistaken. And my name is Miss Taunton, not Eleanor."

I clasped her hand tighter and whispered back. "Oh, Eleanor, I don't care about the paper. Surely you know that? Feel free to give me an F. I want to help you."

Even though she scoffed, she kept her voice down. "Help me? That's rich. Miss Faneuil, you are the one in need of assistance."

"Look at me, Eleanor. You have to forget about George and start fresh. He'll never come back for you. It's been decades. There is hope for a new life for you."

The room was so quiet I could hear the other kids breathe, as they watched us. Still, I was pretty sure they couldn't hear what we were saying.

"How did you know?" she asked, her voice breaking.

The tears that welled in her eyes began to run down her face.

"I saw it in your soul."

Miss Eleanor Taunton put her head down and silently walked out of the room.

THIRTY-SEVEN

So much for hiding in plain sight. Word about my encounter with Miss Taunton spread through the school like wildfire. No one knew what I had said to her, but the kids from my English class definitely saw the tears streaming down her face as she left the room. By the end of second period, the other kids didn't know what to think of me, except that I'd seemingly subjugated the most loathed teacher in school. And they liked that.

The softening in my classmates' attitude toward me made my presence at Tillinghast High School even harder. As I watched the kids take notes in class or laugh with their friends in the hallways or share a cookie over lunch, it reminded me that this could be the last day they did any of these things. That none of us could be here tomorrow if I failed. The frivolities that I'd loathed upon my return from Boston now seemed like innocent indulgences, ones that I'd been charged with protecting.

It was all too much. As the school day came to a close, I needed to rest. I had planned on waiting in the school library for Ruth to finish her yearbook meeting, before we headed together to Michael's championship football game. But I knew that the library—chock-full of flirting kids and studious teens—was like a minefield of sentiment that I could ill afford. In order to protect the kids, I had to be resolute, not emotional, on their behalf.

I needed to be alone. For all those kids' sake, I couldn't allow my resolve to weaken. Against Ruth's protests, I walked out to the parking lot and to my car. I figured that forty-five minutes in the safety of my parents' car to gather my thoughts and muster my courage was in everyone's best interest.

The late afternoon sky had already turned dark and the air cold. Heavy clouds hung in the sky's midlevels and threatened an early snow. Shivering a bit, I wrapped my coat around me and assessed the school grounds. At this time of day, the Tillinghast students' lot was full of cars but nearly devoid of students. They were all hanging out inside the warm school, waiting for the game to start.

The lot felt lonely and exposed, so I hustled over to my car. I opened the door, and then swiftly locked it behind me as I fumbled for the heat. The car slowly warmed, and I allowed myself a deep, calming breath. In the quiet, thoughts of Michael crept into my head. I admonished myself to stay focused, and replayed some of Rafe's tutorials.

As I started to utter a prayer to Him—for the first time, actually—the driver's side window shuddered. I jumped, and reached for the knife in my bag. Then I saw the innocent face of an unfamiliar teenage girl. She knocked gently on the window.

The slightly nerdy blonde, wearing wire-rimmed glasses and carrying a tattered backpack, smiled at me. As I gave her the once-over, checking for any suspicious signs, I noticed that the visitors' parking lot was starting fill up. The girl, who looked lost, was probably from the rival high school.

I rolled down my window a crack. She bent down and asked, "Sorry to bug you . . . do you know where the soccer field is? I've looked everywhere but can't find it."

They were holding a pregame pep rally on the soccer field, which explained the early arrival of so many cars. "Sure. If you go behind the gymnasium, you'll walk right onto it."

She squinted at the school building, and asked, "Which way is the gymnasium?"

I stuck my hand through the window opening, and pointed, "There, that's the—"

The girl grabbed my hand and yanked my arm through

the aperture. Once I was immobilized, she snaked her own arm through the tiny opening and unlocked the door. With unnatural strength, she extricated my arm and dragged me from the car.

With an irritating smirk, she sized me up, and said, "Well hello, Ellspeth Faneuil. It's so nice to finally meet you."

"Who the hell are you?"

"Let's not play games, Ellspeth. I think you know who I am. I'm one of the fallen. My name is Rumiel. We are going to become very good friends."

Rafe was wrong that I'd know the fallen when I saw them. Again.

THIRTY-EIGHT

As I glanced at her face, it morphed the tiniest bit, a transformation so minuscule that an ordinary passerby wouldn't have noticed. Although the blond hair and light brown eyes stayed the same, the innocence disappeared, as did the illusion of youth. I stared into the face of her true, fallen self.

This time I refused to be a victim. I would not even play at being swayed the way I had with Barakel. I wrenched her hand off me, and took to the skies. Never mind who saw.

Time alone in the car had helped immensely; it helped me regain the mental clarity to study the atmosphere and formulate my strategy. I read the wind and understood how to gain speed by maximizing the currents and airflow. I scrutinized the cloud structure and realized that I could use the cover to make my movements hazy and hard to follow.

Within minutes, I saw that Rumiel was having trouble keeping up with me. Whether she was short on practice after all these easy millennia, running the world unchallenged, or whether Rafe's instructions actually were that good, I didn't know. I was thankful. Her inability to keep pace would help me tremendously.

Climbing vertically, I waited until I observed her starting to tire even further. Then I sought out a particularly weighty cloud, one laden with the dark promise of snow. Ducking behind it, I readied my knife and held myself in abeyance until she neared.

I swooped down upon her—slicing her arm with my blade.

Rumiel looked at me aghast. From her shocked expression, I could tell that she couldn't believe that I'd bested her, even if I was prophesied to be the Elect One. But then she realized something more, something that the nature of my attack told her. I knew how to kill her.

She fled.

I could have caught Rumiel instantly. Incredibly, I seemed faster and better at understanding the skies. My strategy, however, didn't include capturing her yet. Instead, I wanted the fallen to exhaust herself and become so weak that I could obtain her blood and deliver the final blow with certainty and ease. I would take no chances.

I stayed in Rumiel's wake. I kept my distance as she wavered in the ocean fog now drifting over land. Temporarily, I spared her, as I watched to see where she would land.

Finally, Rumiel reached the neighboring, rural town of Spaulding. She pursued the destination so doggedly that I wondered whether she had a safe house there, a place where she could hide and nurse her wound. Not that I'd give her the opportunity to recover, mind you.

Even though my body and soul longed to dive down and destroy her—after all, she was responsible for the fifth sign, the persecution of believers—I waited. I lingered in the shelter provided by the fog until she lowered herself to a farm field. It seemed that reaching its picturesque red barn was her real objective.

Rumiel rushed across the remaining yards of the field, and swung open the big barn doors. I waited until the doors banged against the wall behind her, and then I dove down through the fog to reach her side. Without looking around the barn, I grabbed her arm and squeezed hard. I heard her gasp in pain. Looking down at my palm, I saw a few smears of blood. Bracing myself for the revulsion of the act, I licked the blood, shuddering at the bitter, metallic taste.

To my astonishment, Rumiel laughed. Actually laughed as I licked her blood.

"It was worth it to let you drink my blood, so that I could lure you here." She gestured at the barn.

What was so special about this barn that she'd sacrifice her blood to bring me here? I quickly glanced around. There, amid the hay and the cows and goats and farm equipment were my parents. Bound and gagged on the floor.

It was a trap.

As I raced to their sides, I heard Rumiel say, "You see, Ellspeth, I have the unique pleasure of breaking the fifth seal—the persecution of believers. And I thought to myself, what better way to sway young Ellspeth over to my way of thinking before I open the fifth seal than by threatening to persecute some of her favorite believers in Him. At first, I thought I'd use your little friend Ruth. But then I thought of Daniel and Hananel, and I knew they'd serve my purposes a lot better."

While Rumiel giggled to herself, I pulled off my parents' gags and untied the ropes around their wrists and ankles. I asked, "Are you guys okay?"

"We're fine, Ellie. You need to worry about Rumiel. Not us," my mom hurriedly answered, as she and my dad shook their feet and hands back to life.

"What happened to your friends? The Light Fallen, who were supposed to protect you?" I whispered.

"Rumiel killed the six who were guarding us. Including Tamiel." My dad's voice wavered for a moment, then grew stronger. "Don't worry about us, Ellspeth. Kill Rumiel."

Rumiel's voice rang out across the barn. "You're welcome to unbind them, Ellspeth. That won't set them free."

Motioning for my parents to stay in one of the barn's back stalls, I turned around to face my nemesis. Rumiel was no longer alone. Four male Dark Fallen of immense proportions flanked her.

"These fine fellows will be guarding your beloved parents until the end. As long as you act as I say—and, of course, judge the end as I say—they will remain alive. The minute you disobey my instructions, my friends will be happy to strike."

How dare she? How dare she use my parents as pawns in this awful endgame to get at me? My dad's words emboldened me. I would kill Rumiel.

I felt a rage unlike any other ignite within me, and I knew that it would take little for me to channel those flames into the sword of fire. But I couldn't summon the sacred weapon without Michael. Rafe forbade it.

Without an outlet, the rage transmuted. It burned throughout my entire being. Soon, it felt as though the wrath was extinguishing all the humanity in me, leaving only the fire of the angel.

Rafe hadn't told me that this could happen to my body.

Regardless of my parents' presence, I had to act. The fire demanded it. Almost of its own volition, my back expanded with the arc of my wings, and my body lifted into the air. As did Rumiel's. She left her minions to stand guard around my parents.

Across the vaulted ceiling of the barn, I hurtled myself at Rumiel. Her blood made her vulnerable to me, and I wanted to squeeze the life out her with my own hands. As I came within inches of her, I noticed a weapon beneath me. A scythe rested against the stall closest to me.

Instead of finishing her off with my bare hands, I dove down for it. The scythe felt substantial—and pleasing—in my hands. As I approached her again, scythe swinging in my wake, Rumiel smiled.

"You won't do it. You'd risk your parents," she announced with a sickly confident smile. But I noticed hesitation in her eyes.

"You really think I won't, Rumiel? Well, you're wrong. My parents gave me their blessing."

Then I swung the blade. It lodged right into Rumiel's heart. For a seemingly endless moment, she stared at me in disbelief that I'd actually take the chance with my parents so close. As she fell to the hay-strewn barn floor, the life bleeding out of her, her followers scattered to the wind.

It was an act of which I never thought I'd be capable. Despite the prophecy and despite the stakes.

But I had done it. I had killed a fallen. Finally, whether I liked it or not, I felt like the Elect One.

THIRTY-NINE

"Where have you been? I had to fight to keep a seat open for you. The game's already started," Ruth asked, as I sat down on the packed bleacher.

"You don't want to know," I answered, and meant it. I had no intention of revealing the news about Rumiel to the already petrified Ruth, especially since Rumiel had seriously considered kidnapping Ruth and using her as blackmail to sway me. Or worse.

I almost hadn't come to the game. After watching the blood drain from Rumiel's otherworldly body—to make absolutely certain she was dead—the championship football game seemed utterly meaningless. Plus, I was extremely reluctant to leave my parents in the care of the remaining Light Fallen. They had failed to protect my parents before—how could I have confidence that they'd protect them now?

Yet, I knew I should stay near Ruth, after what Rumiel

had threatened. And I felt an undeniable compulsion to be near Michael, even from the distance of a stadium bleacher. I literally had no choice but to heed those calls.

I could tell that Ruth had questions, many questions. She had a right to answers; her life was at risk too, and she knew it. Fortunately, the game had already begun, and the deafening noise prohibited much conversation. To my great relief. I had other work to do.

I needed to focus on the stadium. Not the field where the football game played out but the stands where an end-days battle could transpire. Paramount in my mind were the words spoken by poor Tamiel. She had warned me that the fallen would use any weapon at their disposal to sway me, particularly threats to crowds, to which my sentiments made me particularly susceptible. I couldn't let harm befall my classmates simply because I'd taken the risk of coming to the game. Look what had almost happened to my parents.

I kept my eyes glued on the stands. I observed students and parents from both schools cheering for their respective teams. I watched the popular Tillinghast juniors and seniors cluster together on a remote bleacher as they tried to sneak sips from beers. I noticed a couple kissing in a dark alcove under an awning, much as Michael and I once had.

I discerned nothing unusual. Nothing otherworldly.

Turning my attention to the blur of players on the field, I realized that the Tillinghast coach had called a time-out. The players were huddled on the sideline, listening intently to Coach Samuel's instructions. The whole exchange appeared pretty typical, and I nearly refocused on the stands. Then I noticed the peculiar expression on Michael's face. He looked astonished by whatever play the coach was calling.

The referee's whistle sounded, and Michael quickly hid his reaction. The players clapped, and they started jogging back onto the field. The coach gave Michael one last encouraging slap on the back.

I couldn't take my eyes off Michael as he ran down the field into position. He moved so differently from the other players, so gracefully. So angelically. Watching him made me wistful for what we once shared. I wondered whether we would ever recapture those emotions, whether we would ever be together again. Before . . . or after.

I wondered what had gone wrong between us. It wasn't jealousy of Rafe, although that played no small part. Something had been off for weeks.

As I stared at Michael preparing for whatever play the coach had called, I felt—rather than saw—a pair of eyes on me. I scanned the stands, trying to identify the source. No one seemed to be glancing in my direction, and I started to feel anxious about the odd sensation I was experiencing.

Was there another fallen out there? One I couldn't locate? Then I comprehended that I couldn't pinpoint the person staring at me because I was looking in the wrong place.

I should have been looking on the field.

When I shifted my gaze to the sideline, I locked eyes with a black-haired, blue-eyed man. It was Michael's coach. Obviously, I'd seen him countless times before, at games or practices. But his face had always been shielded by a baseball cap or obscured by sunglasses. I had never had the opportunity to really look at Coach Samuel closely before, and I certainly had never seen him studying me.

At once, I realized that he was a fallen angel. And from the expression on his face, I saw that he realized that I knew his secret.

Suddenly, I knew what had been wrong between me and Michael since we returned from Boston.

FORTY

"Ruth," I whispered, at the same time that something momentous happened on the field, causing the crowd to roar. In the din, she couldn't hear me. "Ruth."

I poked her arm in an effort to get her attention. She mouthed the word "ouch," and rubbed her arm. I started to voice my suspicions to her, yet didn't dare speak very loud. Ruth shook her head in incomprehension.

Pulling my cell out of my bag, I pointed to it. As she reached for hers, I started typing furiously. Then I waited for her reaction.

"The coach is a fallen."

Ruth read the text and froze. When she came to, she stared down at the field, and then whipped her shocked face in my direction for confirmation. I nodded, and she returned to her cell to text a response.

"Let's go get help."

Even without an explanation of "help," I understood her

meaning. She meant that we should seek the assistance of the Light Fallen who were floating around, ostensibly to guard my parents. I knew that they couldn't do anything at all; they were busy trying to keep my parents safe from other threats. But what were our choices? For the millionth time, I wished Rafe hadn't left. He would know exactly what to do.

As we got ready to leave to secure that "help," the crowd got even louder. Ruth took a bit longer than me to gather her belongings, so I glanced down at the field. I was scared to make eye contact with the coach again, even though I wanted to see what the players were doing that had caused such a furor among the fans.

I didn't see the play, but I saw the outcome. In dismay, I watched as Michael fell to the field from the extraordinary height he'd jumped to in order to catch a pass. He fell hard, so hard he wasn't moving. I stared as Coach Samuel, or whatever his real name was, raced onto the field to "aid" his injured star player.

I knew, without a shred of doubt, that the coach had no intention of aiding Michael. That whatever play he had ordered—a play that produced a visceral reaction in Michael the moment he heard it—had the explicit purpose of harming Michael. And that Coach Samuel's ultimate goal in wounding Michael had to involve me in some way.

With a sudden clarity, I understood that Michael had been vulnerable, physically on the field and spiritually for some time. For weeks, the coach had planted seeds of dissension in Michael, nurturing his insecurities and jealousies and doubts and ego with a deft touch. Michael was as susceptible to the coach as he'd been to Ezekiel, although it was a different kind of susceptibility, one so subtle Michael didn't even understand that it was happening.

Coach Samuel was "what had gone wrong" between me and Michael.

Every fiber of my being—human and otherworldly screamed to get down to that field to Michael's side. Knowing that he was in danger was like having my own heart torn from my body. I needed to drag Michael out of this stadium to a place of safety. And I had to get him there before the coach "aided" him any further, by making sure he didn't receive medical care or, worse, sending him back out onto the field with a major injury.

The moment I stood up and raced out of my seat, the entire crowd reacted to another development on the field and stood up as well. I pushed and shoved past all the gaping fans packed into the bleachers in an effort to get onto the field. As I squeezed through the masses, I saw a couple of medics rushing to Michael's side.

I couldn't make a swift escape on foot from the bleachers.

Instinctively, my body readied for flight. If I had to reveal my true nature to save Michael, I would do it. Because all this—the innocence of high school football games; the carefree enjoyment of others' company; even the beauty of a crisp, late fall evening—would vanish if I didn't save Michael and stop Coach Samuel from triggering the next sign. Whatever it was.

Ruth was behind me. She observed the transformation of my body—the expansion of my shoulder blades and the fierce concentration in my eyes. Having secretly watched me and Michael fly, she knew what I was doing. She held me down so I could not get airborne.

"There's another way out," she yelled over the commotion. Pointing to a gap in the crowd, she shouted, "Over there."

If I ran through that gap, I figured that I might make it onto the field in time. On the other hand, if I raced through the hole, I would leave Ruth dangerously exposed as a pawn in Coach Samuel's game.

I looked back at her and mouthed, "What should I do? I don't want to leave you."

She motioned for me to plow ahead, that she would be fine. I hesitated, but she pushed me onward. With her blessing, I dove through the throng.

It was up to me now.

FORTY-ONE

I raced into the break in the crowd and down those stairs faster than Rafe would have believed possible on my earthbound feet. I knew my window of opportunity was extremely small. I had to extricate Michael from the coach's grasp before it was too late.

Pushing past the security guards who were there to control the crowds, I ran onto the field. A swarm of referees and players and medical personnel hovered around the spot where Michael had fallen. I shimmied through a gap, hoping to see an alert Michael in the midst of the masses.

He was gone.

I turned to the referee standing next to me, and yelled, "Where is he? Where is Michael Chase?"

"Miss, you shouldn't be out here. Guards—" he started to shout, before I cut him off.

Grabbing the referee's arm, I commanded, "Tell me where Michael Chase went."

The fight disappeared from his face, and he pointed toward the gateway that led to the locker rooms. "Coach Samuel took him that way, miss. He said a doctor was waiting for them inside."

I dropped his arm and ran toward the locker room, but not before I banged right into the security guards. Unfortunately, the guards had heard the referee's call for help. Taking a page out of Michael's football moves book, I leaped around them with a dose of angelic dexterity, and sped down the long hallway leading to the Tillinghast players' locker room.

Slowing my pace as I reached the heavy door, I listened for sounds of Coach Samuel and Michael. The hallway leading to the locker room was dead quiet, as the team and staff waited out on the field for word from the coach to resume play. Given that, I expected I'd be able to hear something, maybe the coach's footsteps as he carried Michael. Nothing.

I pushed open the locker room door slowly. Wincing at the door's loud groan, I crept into the space and began my search. Although I examined every corner of the labyrinthine room, I didn't see any evidence of them.

Just as I was about to leave, I heard the thud of a closing door. Where had that come from? I was standing before the only door in or out of the locker room that I was aware of. I sprinted to the area from which the sound seemed to originate and discovered what looked like a closet I'd dismissed on my initial investigation. Kicking myself for failing to check it, I turned the handle and braced myself for the otherworldly force within.

Only dirty mops, shelves of cleaning products, and an electrical box stared back at me. Where were Michael and Coach Samuel? Then I spotted it. In the far corner of the dimly lit closet, I could make out the outlines of a narrow door. Dirt smeared, it nearly blended in with the rest of the closet. Nearly.

I pried the handleless door open with my nails. I entered the opening that lurked behind the door. It was fairly dark, with shallow steps, narrow walls, and a low ceiling. It looked like a tunnel. Was this the often rumored about, though never seen, tunnel between the stadium and the high school building?

Something in me immediately recoiled. I couldn't explain why, but the notion of burrowing deep into the earth didn't sit well with me. Maybe because I'd become a creature of the sky.

Despite my revulsion of the deep earth, I propelled myself down the steps into the space. God knows when it had been last used and for what. I had to do it. Michael was somewhere in here. And he needed me more than ever.

Even with the low light from the closet behind me and

the occasional bulb on the ceiling above me, I could tell that the tunnel was too constricted for flight. I had to rely on my human skills; yet even then, the passageway was too dark for running. I scurried as fast as I could in the only direction available to me. Forward. Fear took hold, and I started to worry that this was a trap. Had Coach Samuel planned Michael's injury and this whole escape as a means to lure me to this God-forsaken place?

Within a few minutes, I made out a brighter light ahead of me. The tunnel started to widen, and I was able to pick up speed. I thought I discerned the outline of a figure in the distance. Longing to reach the figure as quickly as possible, and knowing that I still couldn't fly, I began to attempt a projection.

Through the darkness and my own focused thoughts, I heard a voice calling to me. In my shock and terror, I lost the necessary concentration.

"Ellspeth, the space is too narrow for projection. Please do not attempt it. We cannot risk any harm to you, the Elect One."

I froze in fear. The owner of the voice knew who I was and precisely what I was. Whoever was behind that voice could tell exactly what I was doing.

I assumed the voice belonged to Coach Samuel, since it definitely wasn't Michael's. Who else could it be? I was about to call out, when the tunnel abruptly ended. I stood before two narrow passageways, a dark one to my right and a slightly brighter one to my left. Oddly enough, I saw no signs of Michael and the coach. How had they gotten so far ahead of me?

In my split second of hesitation, in that indulgent moment of indecisiveness, a figure emerged from the darkness of the tunnel on the right. And it wasn't Coach Samuel or Michael.

"Samyaza sent me," the figure said, as he swaggered toward me.

Coach Samuel must be Samyaza, I thought. How did I know that name? Then I remembered. Rafe mentioned it when he first told me the story of the fallen and again, when he listed the six Dark Fallen responsible for the end days. Samyaza was the leader of the two hundred angels who descended to earth at His behest to guide humankind, before the angels' fall. And Samyaza was the holder of the seventh seal.

The figure continued his taunt. "Samyaza thought the Elect One might want some company."

FORTY-TWO

"Who are you?" I asked the handsome fallen sauntering toward me, while I tried desperately to keep my voice from quavering.

Even in the dim light, his amber eyes were luminous, and his dark-brown hair lustrous. He was as beautiful as the other fallen I had encountered, although somehow he looked harder and stronger than the rest. Even his clothes—a black leather jacket and boots that had an almost militaristic feel—added to his physical intimidation, not to mention his self-confident swagger. I figured that this smug fallen must serve in the ranks of Coach Samuel, Samyaza I guess I should call him, now that I knew who he truly was.

The fallen answered, "Does it matter, Ellspeth? I've been called by so many names over the millennia. When I first arrived on earth, humankind knew me by one name. Since then, I've been known by so many others. But my real name is Azaziel."

"I'll call you Azaziel, then," I said distractedly. My words were only my currency to buy time. I needed to assess which tunnel held Michael. And how to get rid of this Azaziel in the process.

"My name is not important, as you well know, Ellspeth. All that matters now are the signs. I'm in charge of the sixth. War was always my expertise," he said with an unsettling chuckle.

"War?" Some memory came back to me. Something Rafe had said. But I didn't have time to focus on it. All that I wanted was a few more seconds to determine my course of action.

A distant sound emanated from the brighter tunnel on the left. Michael had to be down there. All I needed to do now was evade this fallen and hasten down that tunnel to Michael's side. Destroying Azaziel would take too much time, precious minutes that rendered Michael more and more vulnerable.

"Yes, I am responsible for the sixth sign. The revolutions. I will be unleashing war soon."

Oh no. With a start, I remembered what Rafe had told me. Azaziel wasn't a minion of Samyaza. Azaziel was one of the key Dark Fallen in the path to the apocalypse. When Michael killed Barakel and I killed Rumiel, the end days timeline had skipped past the fourth and fifth signs to the sixth. We were already at the sign for war.

The knowledge presented me with an impossible situation. I could no longer abandon the task of killing Azaziel so that I could race to rescue Michael. I had to kill Azaziel *and* save Michael or the apocalypse would be upon us. How on earth was I going to do both?

"Samyaza sent me here to impede your progress, to give him more time to prepare for the seventh sign, the final unleashing of our new leader. Our common goal." He smiled. "As usual, Samyaza underestimated me. He didn't think I'd try to sway you myself. He didn't think I'd have time. Fool. He's always been a humankind-loving fool."

The tunnel felt like it was tightening around me, bringing Azaziel dangerously close. I needed to get out of there fast, even though I had no idea where I was going to go or what I was going to do. Although it pained me, although it went against the blood tie Michael and I shared, out of sheer desperation, I dashed past Azaziel into the heart of the dark right-hand tunnel.

I felt, rather than saw, the passageway widen as I entered it. I was able to gain considerable speed and force, enough to allow me to lift off the rough floor and into the air. Azaziel pursued me, as I knew he would. Even though flying through the right-hand tunnel took me farther away from Michael, I needed to get some space between me and

Azaziel to figure out how I was going to kill a fallen angel whose particular expertise was war. Only then, if I came out unscathed, could I return to my hunt for Michael. If it wasn't too late to save him.

We soared and ducked and wove through the increasingly convoluted and surprisingly long tunnel. Much to my own astonishment, I felt like I was outdistancing him, until I felt a burning sensation around my ankle. Still flying as fast as I could, I glanced down.

A whip of bright light had coiled around my ankle, and Azaziel held the other end. It seemed the sword of fire could take many forms, particularly in the hands of the creator of war.

Rafe hadn't prepared me for this.

I reached down to free my ankle, but the cord of light burned my fingertips. I felt Azaziel trying to reel me back with it, like some poor fish on a hook. Although I had no intention of going down quietly, I had absolutely no idea how to unbind my leg.

Without warning, the tunnel emptied out onto a patch of empty countryside. I tumbled down hard upon the ground, and the impact caused the whip to let loose. I stood up and quickly looked around. I couldn't see the high school buildings anywhere. In the background, I heard the crash of the waves. I wondered where I was.

I had no time to speculate before Azaziel raced out of the tunnel. As I took off in the opposite direction of the tunnel, I suddenly placed the sound and locale. I remembered that, before its recent rebuilding, Tillinghast High School used to sit on a hill overlooking the ocean. This was one of the abandoned playing fields that was adjacent to the high school. I used to play here as a kid.

Unexpectedly, the location gave me an idea.

FORTY-THREE

Before I had time to work through my idea, I headed to the nearby coast. As I remembered, there was the rocky shore, topped by a jagged cliff from which a promontory jutted. I flew as fast as my body allowed, yet Azaziel seemed easily able to match my pace.

With the wind at my back, and Rafe's instructions at the forefront of my mind, I gained over Azaziel. I heard the flapping of his jacket in the wind as he raced to catch me. I let the air current take us beyond the rocky beaches over the sea. I continued my trajectory a few moments longer before I flew back to the promontory. In part, I was banking on my more intimate knowledge of this particular coast to gain an advantage. I lower small.

Skirting the single jagged stone that protruded from the hard ridge of rock comprising the promontory, I hovered over the flat center for a second. I stayed long enough for Azaziel to grab my foot and swing me down onto the hard rock. Obviously, his efforts to sway the Elect One weren't going to be gentle. But then, I hadn't expected the angel of war to handle me with kid gloves.

In order to break my fall, I landed on my left hand. The fall left me with a stinging, bloody palm and a gash on my forehead. Pushing myself back up with my uninjured right hand, I struggled to my feet.

We stood within inches of each other on the flat center of the promontory. The waves crashed angrily against the rocks at the promontory's base, some hundred feet below. Up close, Azaziel's beautiful face turned ugly in its mean-ness. I'd never felt so exposed, so at risk. I had to stand my ground or lose my very tiny opportunity.

"Shall I give you a hand, Ellspeth?" Azaziel asked, with a mocking chuckle. He sounded victorious already. I guessed that Azaziel hadn't seen much in the way of defeat over the millennia.

Before I could answer or take to the sky, he seized my bloody left hand, grinning when I winced in pain. Azaziel was practically beaming in delight at the prospects of swaying me through his ancient, powerful touch. He clearly could not imagine a scenario in which he did not succeed.

As he dug his fingers deeper and deeper into my raw palm, I got a flash into the inequity and vice of Azaziel's soul. He spent his long, long years on earth taking out his anger at God on the minds and bodies and spirits of men through relentless warfare. Every human whipped into a hostile battlefield frenzy was another victory to be flaunted at Him. Azaziel coveted control over me—and the ensuing control over the end days—so he could magnify his domination.

I felt no compunction whatsoever about killing him. Did I have the bravery and physical prowess? With Barakel, I'd proven to myself that I had the mental fortitude to fend off the fallen's wiles, and with Rumiel, I'd proven that I had the physical power to destroy. I prayed directly to Him for more of both. Because Barakel and Rumiel paled in comparison to Azaziel as adversaries.

A rope of light formed in Azaziel's free hand. As he wrapped it around my wrists, his fingers grazed my skin, and he started to transmit thoughts to me through his touch—messages about the end days and the necessity of following his lead. The part of me still able to think clearly got really, really scared. How was I going to free myself from Azaziel and his cord of light before I lost my remaining will?

A mad idea came to me.

Instead of wresting my wrists from the rope, I pressed the rope deep into my bleeding palm. The burning was almost intolerable at first, and I nearly let go. But then I sensed the power of the otherworldly light—the power summoned from Azaziel's own core—surging into my body.

Who said a half angel could never have the might of a full angel?

With the ease of Azaziel's borrowed strength, I broke the rope. Azaziel froze in astonishment. I could almost hear his thoughts: There was no way a stupid teenage girl—prophesied Nephilim or not—could best the creator of war.

I flew in a vertical line directly above the sharp point of the promontory. Azaziel came for me. Faster than I expected. And with more hatred in his eyes than I believed possible. I knew then that he would kill me if he could.

Rather than flying away from him as he approached, as every fiber of my being screamed at me to do, I rushed toward him. With my newfound strength, I grabbed his arm and shoved him directly into the promontory's razor-like point.

Azaziel wasn't used to suffering injuries; he was only used to inflicting them. I dipped my finger in the blood flowing from his wound, and then into my mouth, before I shoved him into the promontory point again. His eyes flickered in disbelief even as the life drained from his body.

The pride I'd counted on—the pride Rafe described to me—served me well.

This time, unlike after the destruction of Rumiel, I couldn't watch to ensure that I'd destroyed the fallen. I had to find Michael.

FORTY-FOUR

One fallen remained. One sign left. And Michael.

Would I make it in time to kill the fallen, stop the sign, and save Michael? Or would I be forced to choose?

I had to go back into the same dark tunnel that had dumped me onto these neglected playing fields. I had to retrace my route through the subterranean warren for which my sky-bound body was so ill fitted. How else would I find Michael?

Though I shuddered at the thought of reentering the tunnel, I braced myself for the inevitable. I tore my eyes from the body of Azaziel splayed across the rock beneath me. As I accelerated through the crisp night air toward the mouth of the tunnel, I could tell that my body was hurt and fatigued. Fortunately, adrenaline pumped through me at such a rate I could hardly feel my hurt hand, my bruises, or my exhaustion. I had to save Michael.

I slowed my pace only to better navigate through the

passageway. Then I immediately picked up as much speed as possible. Just as the tunnel started to constrict a little, I saw light in the distance. I knew I had to be getting closer to the brighter of the two tunnels—the one into which I was certain Michael and Samyaza had escaped.

I reached the place where the three tunnels first met. As I made the turn into the mouth of the tunnel, it tapered down. There was no hope of flight, so I lowered myself to the ground.

The air was so still I could barely breathe, but I knew I could bear it, if each step deeper underground brought me closer to Michael. I replayed images of Michael in the high school hallways and at the Odeon theater on our first date and in the night sky, as if the memories would shorten my journey to his side. Remembrances of the real Michael, not the Michael he had become under Samyaza's influence. Anything to propel my slow, earthly legs faster.

When I thought I couldn't bear another moment without the wind and the sky and the stars, the tunnel ended. The rough earth floor gave way to familiar linoleum, and ceramic tiles now lined the walls. The close, dank air dissipated, and a recognizable scent—chemical, though not unpleasant—filled the space. A soft, hazy light appeared. I heard the muffled sounds of cheering.

The floor, the walls, the smell, the sound. Suddenly,

I knew where I was. The basement of Tillinghast High School.

I stood at the end of a long hallway. Illumination leaked from the outline of a closed door to my left. Instinct told me that my poor wounded Michael, maybe bleeding, maybe near death, was behind that door. Samyaza along with him.

I couldn't wait to punish Samyaza for all the problems he'd caused between me and Michael and for all his grand designs to break the seventh seal. I was sick of the fallen and their apocalyptic games. For the first time, instead of fear at the confrontation I undoubtedly faced, I felt exhilaration.

I couldn't wait to kill Samyaza.

FORTY-FIVE

I shoved open the door and was met by black hair, bright blue eyes, and an eager smile. There, in the shadows of a subterranean den of my nightmares, awaited Samyaza, the last of the Dark Fallen.

His arms opened and reached out to embrace me. "Ellspeth, my darling. I have long envisioned our reunion." His voice was warm, almost loving.

Our "reunion?" What was he talking about? I'd gotten accustomed to fallen angels extolling their long years of pining to meet me, but a reunion? We needed to have a first meeting before he could long for a second. The only time I'd ever encountered Samyaza was near the football field—during a game or at practice—and then, he only had eyes for his star player, Michael. I'd hardly categorize this as a long-awaited "reunion."

My confusion was clearly written on my face, and Samyaza spoke again. "You wouldn't remember the first time we met, Ellspeth. You were only hours old. Even then, you were beautiful," he said, tears of happiness welling in his eyes. Tears that seemed real.

What was going on? Why would Hananel and Daniel let Samyaza near me when I was a helpless, newborn baby? It didn't make any sense. Unless it wasn't my adoptive mom and dad who let Samyaza near me. Unless he was already with me when they arrived to take me away, because he'd been at my actual birth.

"I've been looking for you ever since. And not because you are the Elect One."

I knew what Samyaza was going to say next before he even said it. "Because you are my daughter, Ellspeth."

I needed only to look at him, with his jet-black hair and the pale blue eyes so like my own, to know that it was true. Samyaza—leader of the fallen since the beginning of time and the holder of the seventh seal—was my father.

I was so confused. Standing before me was the father I'd envisioned since I learned who I really was. I had so many questions for him. I wanted to know about my mother, about their relationship, about what had happened to me. I felt my carefully constructed veneer of strength eroding and my will to fight sapping away.

I couldn't let that happen. No matter who Samyaza was, my mission was clear. I had to save Michael, and stop the seventh seal.

"Where is he? Where is Michael?" I asked. I willed my voice to sound strong and unflinching, even though I certainly didn't feel that way.

"He is here, Ellspeth. And he is well."

"Why should I believe you?"

Samyaza actually looked offended. "I would never, ever hurt him. Just as I would never, ever harm you. I know how much Michael means to you, and I would never cause you the pain of his loss."

His voice sounded sincere. But I couldn't trust him. Other fallen had tried to hurt me before.

"Is that why you ordered that last play, knowing that it would injure him? Tell me where he is," I said.

"Ellspeth, I ordered that play because it was the only way to orchestrate this meeting in the time we had left," Samyaza said quietly. And then he smiled. He looked like an indulgent parent patiently sitting out his child's tantrum, while waiting for the perfect teaching moment.

Michael stepped out from the shadows.

"I'm here, Ellie. Samyaza is right. I'm fine."

Michael drew closer to me, as if to prove his well-being. I saw no sign of the injuries from the field. I was about to link arms with him in preparation for slaying the last fallen, when a troubling thought entered my consciousness. Michael had called him Samyaza.

Taking one step nearer me, Michael placed his palms

on my cheeks. "Ellie, it's time."

Time for what? I was confused and irritated at this mention of time. Yet, after all the troubles that had passed between us—jealousies and arguments and Rafe and even football—his loving touch felt so wonderful, so reassuring. I almost gave up my inquisitiveness and my fight. Almost. Shades of Ezekiel passed through my mind. Had Michael become an automaton to Samyaza, as he had with Ezekiel? And was he trying to loop me in?

"No, Michael." I withdrew in horror. "You promised me. You promised that this would never happen again."

"Look at me, Ellie. I am not the creature I became with Ezekiel."

I thoroughly examined him. Michael was right. He wasn't in some glassy-eyed, trancelike state as he'd been with Ezekiel. In fact, he positively glowed with alert healthiness. Still, he *was* different. Indescribably so.

"What have you done to him?" I turned to Samyaza.

"Ellspeth, my darling, I have not done anything to Michael. I have explained to Michael who he is, that's all."

Again, this sounded uncannily like our exchange with Ezekiel. "We know who we are. We are the Nephilim, here to destroy the fallen," I answered, and then added, "which includes you."

"My darling, darling child. You are so much more than

mere Nephilim. You and Michael are—" Samyaza said.

"Ellie, there is a reason that two Nephilim are mentioned in the prophecy," Michael interjected. Although all this reeked of our last moments with Ezekiel, Michael's commanding tone told me that he was no puppet of Samyaza's. What the hell was going on? "We each have a special role to play."

"My darling Ellspeth," Samyaza continued for him, "you are the Elect One, as you know. You will judge every earthly creature when the last seal is broken. After you do so—when you fairly judge all earthbound beings in the manner I pray you will—Michael will lead the earth's new order."

Bells were ringing in my mind. The seventh sign. The emergence of a leader after the apocalypse, an anti-Messiah, according to some accounts.

Samyaza meant Michael to be that seventh sign.

FORTY-SIX

No, no. Not my Michael. He couldn't mean Michael.

"Don't you see, my darling Ellspeth? You are the Elect One, and Michael is the seventh sign. Together we will rule the new world, and together we will make it a wondrous place."

I saw, all right. I saw that, since we had returned from Boston, Samyaza had preyed upon the very flaw that would transform Michael. The very flaw that plagued the original angels sent by God. The very flaw that Samyaza had in droves. Pride.

Glancing at Michael, I saw precisely what was different about him. He was practically alight with pride at the promise of leading the world. And not just serving as the "knight" to the Elect One.

I said nothing. I was trying to process it all and still maintain some semblance of myself. Who was this being who called himself my father?

Samyaza walked toward me. His bright, pale blue eyes brimmed with pity and gentleness. The empathy and understanding was so intense I couldn't break his gaze. "My darling child, I know this is difficult and perplexing. You've been led to believe that I am the enemy. I am not who you think I am, and the new world order I've dreamed about need not be the hellacious universe rife with corruption and greed and violence you've seen in the flashes from my fellow fallen. I am not like the other fallen, and the earth we create will be different from the one fashioned by the other fallen in the years since we tumbled from grace. It will be good."

I saw that Samyaza believed the words he said. He *was* different from the other fallen I'd encountered. But what was this universe he envisioned? What was his conception of good?

My face must have revealed my bewilderment, because Samyaza chose that moment to reach out and touch me. He conveyed startling, breathtaking images to me. I saw a time and place, so unknown and unknowable that it could only be the beginning. I saw Samyaza's exquisite face, staring into the adoring eyes of a young woman. I saw that Samyaza delighted in her innocence and relished the wonder in her eyes when he taught her the secrets of the earth and sky. I saw the moment when the fallen fell, the moment when my parents became one, the moment of my birth.

The images brought so many questions to my mind. I observed the rush of emotion Samyaza felt for me as an infant. How did he ever let me fall out of his control as a baby? Had my birth mother somehow come to know Daniel and Hananel, and Samyaza lost me through that connection? Given the ban on fallen angels procreating, how had Samyaza and my birth mother managed to create me?

Samyaza released my hand, and asked, "Do you see, my darling Ellspeth?"

"I do see, Samyaza." I saw that my father indeed loved my mother in his way, as my parents had told me. And I saw that he loved me too. The images were so powerful, so very personal that I started to cry. Michael reached over to give me a consoling hug, even though he wasn't privy to the flash I'd experienced.

Samyaza looked relieved. "You do see, my darling girl, don't you? You witnessed the love I have for humanity. Do you see that the Maker is wrong? What harm is there in revealing our celestial knowledge to humans? What is so terrible about what the fallen did at the beginning? It isn't evil to love and celebrate humankind, as we did in the beginning and as I would continue to do. It isn't wrong to share the secrets of the universe with them. It is good.

God's hubris alone tells us we can only love and honor Him. His hubris alone caused the fallen to fall."

He paused, and then said, "Ellspeth, we have a chance at a new beginning. Together, we can create a new world honoring humankind. Father and daughter."

Father and daughter. The words sounded so very appealing, so very tempting. I stared at Samyaza, unable to forget the images of his euphoric face as he stared into the eyes of his infant daughter—me. I wanted so much to join him, to link hands with my birth father and surrender the lonely job that I'd been given.

A job that suddenly seemed riddled with uncertainty, because I didn't believe that Samyaza was evil. Had I been on the wrong side all along? Maybe the fallen did the right thing in disobeying God. After all, they taught humankind so many good things along with the bad. And why should knowledge and love be a sin?

Good and evil started to appear not so black-and-white. Without that conviction, how could I kill Samyaza, my father?

I felt myself being won over by his emotions and his logic. My lips parted, and I almost, almost said yes.

But I couldn't ignore the echo of Rafe's voice in my mind and the certainty I'd felt listening to his words. I couldn't disregard the evil I had seen in the other fallens' souls. I couldn't overlook the fact that Michael was turning into a benign tyrant—a version of Samyaza—right before me. And most of all, I couldn't close my eyes to certain troubling images I'd seen in Samyaza's flash, images to which he was blind.

Samyaza truly believed that he acted out of love for humankind, because he treated them with kindness and respect. In truth, however, he understood little about loving others. He loved himself—his godlike power to create and rule supreme over others—and the reflected love he saw in humans' eyes. Samyaza served his ego, not humankind and certainly not God. Evil took many forms. That was the nature of Samyaza's grave sin of pride.

The beautiful vision Samyaza showed me and described to me was flawed. Although it broke my heart, I knew what I had to do. Rafe had already forewarned me. But I had no idea that it would be *this* hard.

Michael was still standing next to me. I clasped his hand. "Do you still love me?" I asked him.

"More than ever."

I searched his eyes, and saw that his feelings for me were indeed strong and true. Whether those emotions were tainted by his excitement over the prospect of his new role—and the notion of us ruling the earth together— I couldn't tell. I had to take a leap of faith that his love for me would trump his pride. Because I couldn't do what I needed to do unless Michael had my back.

"Do you believe that I act for good?"

Even though he arched his eyebrow quizzically at the question, he answered confidently, "Yes, Ellie. I do."

"Do you trust me, Michael?"

"Always, Ellie."

"If I promise to follow your lead afterward, will you promise to follow my judgment now?"

He hesitated for a split second, and then responded, "Yes. I promise."

I had to trust him, hesitation or not.

"Please come with me," I said.

Hand in hand, we crossed the short distance to Samyaza. I came within inches of him. Staring up close at his pale blue eyes, jet-black hair, and fair skin, so like mine, I couldn't speak. I knew that, if I opened my mouth, I might soften And I could not afford to weaken.

I released Michael's hand, and extended my right arm. Closing my eyes, I concentrated with the core of my being and envisioned a stream of light emanating from my hand. I felt heat radiating from my fingertips, and then opened my eyes. The sword of fire formed in my hand.

The blade of fire hovered near Samyaza. My father. The last of the apocalyptic fallen.

I didn't know if I could do it, even though I knew I had to. Samyaza didn't flinch at my advance. Instead, he looked into my eyes. He gazed at me with a deep and abiding love.

"Whatever you do, Ellspeth, I will accept your decision. I promised your mother on her deathbed that, when this moment came, as we knew it would, I would not resist. Please remember that I will always love you. As I loved your mother. And as I love all humankind."

Tears streamed down my face. How could this possibly be the right decision? I saw love on my father's face, flawed though it might be. My blade flickered and quivered at my vacillation.

I felt Michael's fingers close around mine. Quickly glancing at him, I saw no more hesitation. I saw that the light of pride in his eyes was extinguished, only to be replaced by a pure flame of love and faith. For me.

He whispered, "I love you, Ellie, and I promised to follow you. This is your judgment. Now is the moment. You must do it now. Only you can."

Michael kept his vow. Even though that oath forced him to sacrifice the role of leading humankind—and his pride. He did it for humankind and for me. His surrender gave me the final bit of courage and conviction that I so desperately needed.

I knew that I had no choice. I only needed to lift my

sword. I did not even have to taste Samyaza's blood before I acted. His blood already ran in my veins.

The sword felt heavy in my hand as I raised it before the final fallen. Samyaza, the father I would never know, did not avert his eyes. With patience and surrender, he awaited my verdict.

I brought the blade within inches of his neck. Then I begged, "Forgive me, Father."

FORTY-SEVEN

The world went black. The earth shuddered beneath my feet, and then cracked wide open. I plunged into a void. My entire being spiraled into a vortex seemingly without end.

Yet I felt no fear. Where I was, what fate would befall me, mattered not at all.

For I had failed. I had no memory of killing my father, Samyaza. No clear recollection of using the sword of fire upon him. The last thing I remembered was the blade hovering over his neck and my uncertainty at delivering the blow.

I had not destroyed the final fallen before Samyaza unleashed the seventh seal—Michael—upon the world. I had not fulfilled the prophecy. I had abandoned my parents, Ruth, and all humankind to a horrific fate.

The blackness, the shuddering, the void, this had to be the abyss of hell. I deserved it. I shut my eyes and surrendered to the oblivion.

It was short-lived. Without warning, my feet hit earth. I felt a soft, gritty substance under my shoes. Behind my closed lids, I sensed light. I dared to open my eyes.

I stood before the most magnificent ocean I had ever seen. The sea was rich indigo, capped by vast, cresting waves. The grainy material beneath my feet was fine, white sand. On the horizon, the sun was beginning its ascent, and soft golden light began to illuminate the shore. I realized that somehow I had landed on a glorious beach beyond my wildest imaginings.

Except the scene evoked the imaginings of my visions. Almost uncannily so.

Suddenly, I appreciated that I was not alone. My hand was linked with that of another.

I turned to see white blond hair, pale green eyes, and a familiar, beautiful face. My Michael. Here, with me. Not side by side with Samyaza, leading their new world order. What had happened? I thought that I had failed. I was *certain* that I had failed.

I turned to him hesitantly. "Where are we?"

"We are at Ransom Beach."

As soon as he spoke, the ocean, the shoreline, and the cliff at our back became very recognizable. The cove had initially appeared different only because it looked brighter.

"Why does it look so different?"

"Do you remember some of the passages from the Book of Enoch that Ruth read to us? It said that, when the Elect One issues the final judgment, when the Elect One stops the end days desired by the fallen, it will change the face of heaven and the face of earth. Based on Ransom Beach, it looks like your act changed the face of the earth."

He confused me. What did he mean?

Very gently, very lovingly, Michael placed his hands upon my shoulders and looked into my eyes. "You did it, Ellie."

"I did?"

"Yes, Ellie. We were transported here when you killed Samyaza before he unleashed the seventh sign upon the earth. Me," he said sheepishly, even apologetically. "You used the sword of fire."

I didn't know how to feel. If I had truly succeeded, if I had actually managed to summon the courage to slay the last fallen and rouse Michael to his calling, the victory was somewhat bittersweet. Imbedded within that triumph was the knowledge that I had killed my birth father. A creature who had loved humankind—and me—albeit in his imperfect way.

I tried to remind myself that the sacrifice was necessary. It had allowed me to rescue the world from the darkness Samyaza would have undoubtedly inflicted upon humankind through his misguided intentions. And give this to the world instead.

"I don't remember, Michael. I don't remember using the sword of fire on Samyaza." I couldn't bring myself to call him "my father." It was too fresh a wound.

Michael observed the mixed emotions in my eyes and rushed to reassure me. "You did, Ellie. Together we did what we were born to do. You embraced your full nature and power, instead of hiding behind the facade of a regular girl. I relinquished my hurt pride at not being the Elect One. We stopped the seventh sign. We stopped the end days."

I gazed into his eyes, and I perceived the truth of his words.

Michael leaned his forehead against mine. For a long moment, we just breathed. Breathed the fresh air of freedom around us. Breathed the sweet relief of each other's presence. Then he touched his lips to my own.

It was a kiss unlike any other we had shared. Perfect, complete unto itself. No wish for his blood. There was no longer any need, it seemed.

"I love you, Ellie."

"I love you too, Michael."

The moment and my vision became one.

With one exception.

After Michael and I broke our embrace to gaze at the

bright new world around us, I noticed something. In the far distance, through the filter of a filmy cloud lingering on the edge of the horizon, I thought I saw a distinctive form. I squinted through the mounting brightness of the rising sun, trying to discern the shape. For a fleeting second, the figure materialized.

Broad shoulders; brown hair and eyes; and a wry, knowing smile. It was Rafe.

He was watching me. Watching us. For all eternity.

ACKNOWLEDGMENTS

The Fallen Angel series would never have taken flight if not for the encouragement of so many people. I must start by thanking my wonderful agent Laura Dail, who cheered me onto this new venture into the young adult realm and offered invaluable guidance. I would also like to express my appreciation to the fantastic team at HarperTeen, including Elise Howard, Farrin Jacobs, Zareen Jaffery, Sarah Landis, Catherine Wallace, Rose Carrano, Becki Heller, the art department, the promotion and sales departments, and the managing editorial and production departments. And I am so thankful for the Pittsburgh book community of libraries, bookstores, book clubs, reporters, and especially readers.

My extended family and friends provided enthusiasm along the way, including but by no means limited to: my parents, Coleman and Jeanne Benedict; my siblings, Coley, Liz, Lauren, Sean, Courtney, Christopher, and Meredith, and their wonderful families; my in-laws, particularly Catherine Terrell and Alison Lichtenberger; Illana and Sophia Raia; Ponny Conomos Jahn ("my pilot light"); the Six; and Mary Zeleny.

But the people most deserving of thanks are my husband, Jim, and our sons, Jack and Ben. Truly, they make *everything* in my world possible, far beyond the Fallen Angel series or anything else I can dream up. Thank you, thank you, thank you.